Project Wormwood

L. D. Nelson

Integrity Publishing

Project Wormwood

 Published by Integrity Publishing, 6117 Brockton Ave., Suite 105 Riverside, CA 92506.

Cover design by Arron D. Nelson Jr.

Edited by Katie M. Toman, Arron D. Nelson Jr., and Arron D. Nelson Sr.

Printed in the United States of America

Categories: 1. Fiction 2. Mystery
3. Politics 4. Religion
5. Government 6. Thriller

Dedication

I'm dedicating this book to my beloved wife Kathleen. Without her unconditional love, devotion and uncompromising support, I could never have become all I am today.

I give all my glory and honor to my Lord Jesus Christ who found me when I was just a boy. He developed, matured, blessed me, and gave me grace and favor for over 50 years. Without him I could surely have not have written this book.

And to my son, Arron and two daughters, Roxy and Wendy, who gave me constant encouragement, along with all my grandchildren. Thank you so much, I love you all.

And last but not least, a very dear friend, Guy Walsh, who was my first pastor, mentor and dear friend. Thank you Doctor Walsh for all you taught me about service to Christ.

Project Wormwood

Prologue: When I began to write this book, I was determined to present an accurate account of the story I am about to tell as possible without revealing any classified information of the Russian or United States Government, or revealing any personal identities. However, upon the near completion of my manuscript I lost control of it to some unnamed persons, and it was sent to a member of The United States State Department without my knowledge or consent.

Four weeks after the computer disk containing my unfinished work was covertly taken from my office, I received a large brown envelope in the Special Delivery mail at my home in Moscow. There was no return address on it but inside I discovered to my dismay it was from the U.S. State Department. It contained an introduction and a lengthy letter from a person I shall call Rudy. It also contained my incomplete manuscript typed out on plain white copying paper, but my computer disk was not in the envelope.

The letter was written in very forceful language, which in part, strongly suggested that I obscure and change the locations and even the names of some of the cities that I had depicted in my manuscript, and to change the names of all the primary characters. It was even strongly suggested that I destroy my manuscript altogether, and not submit it to any publisher. To do so and have it published I may be compromising the national security interests of the whole western world. If I cooperate I will be fully compensated for all my efforts thus far. But if I do seek to have it published without making the changes the letter suggested, they will prevent the publication of my manuscript in any of the Western countries or European countries. The world court may even consider legal action against me.

Although I am vehemently against any kind of government censorship I feel I must comply with their directive if I want to get this story out to the general public. And now that the locations of places, names of cities have been changed or altered, my work has become fictitious and most of the primary characters names have been changed, I leave it to my readers to draw their own conclusions. Is it fact or fiction?

As I begin to tell the story I urge my readers to keep in mind that after many extensive interviews with the primary character of whom this story portrays it was impossible to know what some of the intermediate characters had said or thought. So in order to create a story that was both harmonious and interesting, I, as the author, took literary license to fill in with conjecture what we were unable to discover from the intermediate characters. I can assure you that these various conjectures on my part were carefully and consistently used through learning of the character and circumstances pertaining to each of the intermediate characters after many extensive interviews with those who are still alive.

Chapter 1

As the early morning sun rose lazily over the horizon on that crisp cold October morning, it appeared as a thin crescent of fire lying on the valley floor, to the driver of the big black sedan as he cautiously ambled down the side of the mountain road. A lone passenger in the rear seat was looking out the window with a deliberate gaze toward the mountains, as if he was expecting to see something that his driver was not aware of. The passenger, Erik Roskov, could not in a thousand lifetimes have imagined the chain of events that was about to take place, that would alter his life and so many others forever.

Erik's gaze out of the window was broken by a soft voice from his driver, "Boss, I can see the smoke from the cabin it looks like we are about 5 1/2 kilometers away." Erik leaned forward to get a better look down the mountain road.

"Pull the car over to the side Sid, I want to take a look around before anyone discovers we are here." Sid, the driver steered the sedan over to the side of the road and stopped, he knew when his boss gave an order that it was not a suggestion, and it was to be carried out promptly.

Erik opened the rear passenger side of the sedan and paused without getting out, he began to scan the horizon on his side of the mountain; and as though talking softly to an unseen person he said, "They have got to know we are here by now."

Erik had received a phone call last night informing him that Mrs. Gertrude (Greta) Burkov, one of the principle members of a secret project, the same secret project that he was sent from England to investigate, was in a cabin in the mountains just two hours from Moscow. He was instructed to be at the cabin first thing in the morning and take her into custody, then send her to England for questioning. It was an overseas call from Mr. O'Donnell, who also cautioned Erik that the Russian Military may also try and abduct the target, to keep her from falling into the hands of British Intelligence. Erik responded by sending an agent to watch the cabin and to contact him if the occupant left. Then he called his driver Sid and instructed him to pick him up at 5:00 A.M. to drive him to the cabin.

This was Sid's passenger whom he respectfully referred to as, "Boss," Erik Roskov was about 6 feet tall with red hair that was so tightly woven into small curls it could be easily mistaken as a manufactured hairpiece. He was not movie star handsome, and he was rugged in his appearance with his full thick red eyebrows and the furrows carved in his brow. His laugh lines, which were prominent on his light complexioned face, gave him the look of a father who had just caught his teen age son smoking behind the barn. Giving him that scowling look of displeasure and disappointment combined. He was so serious one had to wonder why he had laugh lines at all, since he so seldom even smiled. When he did arrange a rare smile his face appeared to be in severe pain. His camouflage military jacket lay on the seat next to him. He was dressed in full camouflage military fatigues with a leather holster strapped just below his left armpit resting snuggly against his massive rib cage, and inside the holster was a Russian-made 38 caliber automatic pistol in a 45 frame A weapon of choice that he always had with him since his Uncle Jerrod Stevens gave it to him when he turned eighteen years old. At that time he was living with his uncle in England, where he was attending school. Beside him on his jacket were two full clips of live ammunition.

Cautiously putting one foot outside on the ground and raising a pair of binoculars he held in one hand. He turned and stood erect while placing his forearms on the top of the sedan for support of the binoculars. Then in one quick motion placed his other foot outside the car and firmed it up on the ground; now he was standing in a spread eagle position carefully scanning every inch of the horizon over the mountains. Down the road into the valley, Erik could now see the plumes of light gray smoke curling up from the mountain cabin that was yet just outside his range of vision, but he did not see any sign of the Russian military.

Erik climbed back inside the car and closed the door, then he said to Sid, "Continue driving down the road for another three or four kilometers and try to find a place to pull the car off the road, so it will be hidden from the air, and from anyone driving by on the road."

"I know just the place," Sid said as he pulled the sedan back onto the road.

Sid then pulled a small slim cigar from his shirt pocket and placed it in his mouth. As he engaged the cigar lighter in the car, he heard Erik from the rear seat say, "If you're going to smoke that stinking thing, roll up the glass between us, and turn on the circulating air." Sid had momentarily forgotten after these five years he had served his boss that he could not tolerate the smell of a cigar.

He quickly engaged the air and rolled up the glass that separated the driver's seat of the sedan from the rear passenger seat, and spoke into the car's intercom in an apologetic voice, "Sorry boss I wasn't thinking."

Sid Kachinski was opposite in almost every way to Erik. He was born to very poor parents in the Russian city of

Minsk, he never completed elementary school and lacked the social skills of even the Russian lower class. His father had left him and his mother when he was only five years old and they never saw or heard from him since. When Sid was 12 years old, he and his mother moved to the city of Moscow and shared a small one-room apartment with a black man who she called Ray. He and Sid did not get along from the very beginning. Ray was an American, and that may have been the cause of much of their troubles. When Sid was 15 years old he left his mother's apartment and lived on the streets of Moscow. He ran small errands for some undesirable people that he met just to earn a few rubles to eat on. After two years on the streets he was "streetwise," he began to hang around the bars and the "pleasure rooms." He was not in the least a handsome man, he was small framed, slender and about 5'8" tall with very little hair on top of his head. What little hair he had was combed neatly across the top of his head in a cornrow fashion. There was a narrow band of jet black hair curling around his head from one ear to the other only slightly widening at the back of his head where it sloped down to the top of his collar, like a hill that had been recently graded.

Contrasting that with Erik Roskov, the man now sitting in the rear seat of the sedan, of which Sid had worked for and been a close companion for the last five years, Erik was born into an affluent family. Member of Soviet aristocracy who enjoyed all the privileges that most Russian families could only dream of. He was educated in a private military school in England and then attended Oxford University. He received degrees in both chemistry and political science in only three years. His father was a member of the Politburo and held several high offices in the Soviet government and he was also a retired three star general in the Soviet military. Erik was slightly younger than Sid, he was 28 while Sid was 34. Erik's rugged good looks and full head of curly red hair attracted many women, but he was not interested in any kind of a relationship. He was totally committed to his work, and had been all the five years Sid had known him.

As Sid drove the sedan slowly down the mountain road he glanced up into the rearview mirror only to see his boss carefully perusing a crude map that he held on his lap. Erik glanced up and made a gesture with his right hand as though he was fanning unseen tobacco smoke away from his face. Sid knew he had better get rid of his cigar, so he rolled down his window about half way and tossed a nearly full cigar out onto the roadway and rolled it up again. Without thinking, Sid made a grimacing face and scowled as he raised his eyes to the rearview mirror, and just as quickly he reshaped his face to normal hoping his boss was still looking down at his map. He thanked God he didn't see him.

Studying the map that had led him to this mountain road, on which the small cabin lay just ahead of him, Erik turned his thoughts to his beloved mother who had been diagnosed with a terminal cancer just as he was leaving Oxford University in England. When he was just 20 years old he had completed his high school and vocational education at a private English military school located in the city of Sussex, and then he went to Oxford University. He was sent to England when he was 12 years old, he could well remember that day when his mother and father bid farewell to him at the air terminal in St. Petersburg Russia. He could remember thinking why? Why must I leave our home in Russia to go and live with an uncle in England whom I had never met? Weren't there some fine private military schools in Russia where I could be close to my beloved mother and father? He remembered that he never asked that question then or sense then. For his father always made all the decisions in the family and no one, not he or his mother would ever say or do anything that would question a decision his father made.

His mother chose to remain in the main terminal area of the airport that day, after saying goodbye and giving him a tight hug and kiss. He and his father walked hand-in-hand toward the boarding gate. As they arrived at the gate he tried to hold back tears as he said goodbye to his father, but as the boarding began he found it was impossible too. A small stream of tiny tears began to make their way out of his eyes, and began slowly cascading down his little boy cheeks. Though he tried very hard to hold them back he was unable too. His father turned and looked into his son's face and he saw the look of embarrassment. Without uttering a word he took his little boy's face into his massive strong hands and brushed back the tears then said, "It will be fun, and a good experience for you to live with your uncle while you attend school in England." With those last words his father took him by the hand and they walked together up the boarding ramp into the plane.

His father was right, it was fun living with his uncle. But, for those eight years he missed being with his mother and father so very much. He looked forward to the few visits he had with his father when he would travel to England on state business, and he would always reserve at least a couple of days to stop in and visit with his son at the military school in Sussex and also at Oxford University. Eric longed to see his beloved mother whom he had not seen for the entire eight years he was in England.

When Erik was 20 years old, remembering as though it was yesterday, he returned to his uncle's house from Oxford, two days before graduation. His uncle gave him the telegram he had received that morning from his father in Russia. Mama was diagnosed with cancer, she's okay, attend graduation ceremonies and return home, “Stop.” She can't wait to see you. “Stop.” Get money from Uncle Jerrod and I will repay. “Stop.” Book the next flight home after graduation. “Stop.” Love Mama and Papa.

He was glad he had finished his exams, because he couldn't focus his mind on studying after he got the news about his mother. He attended his graduation ceremony as his father had instructed and said goodbye to a few close friends. With a very emotional parting from his Uncle Jerrod, he boarded a plane at the London Heathrow Airport destined for his beloved mother and father in Moscow.

He was no longer the 12-year-old child that he was when he left Russia for England, he was a grown man now ruggedly handsome and 6 feet tall. Although his mother had seen pictures of him she had not been able to hold her grown son in her arms for eight long years. Not since has she held him so tight as though she could not let go of him at the airport in St. Petersburg, Russia eight years ago.

The flight from London to Moscow seemed like an eternity, because Erik could not get his mind off the telegram he had received, telling of his beloved mother’s sickness. As the big jumbo jet touched down ever so gently on the runway at the Moscow international terminal, Erik's mind was distracted from his mother long enough for him to think of all the important changes that had taken place in this country since he left for England eight years ago. The old guard was almost all gone and a new and younger, more democratic form of government had taken its place under the leadership of President Putin. The war in Afghanistan was all but forgotten, and the war against the breakaway regime in Chechnya was under negotiations to bring about a peaceful solution. So many changes had taken place in his own life as well. The most significant being that he was now a special agent for the British Intelligence Service, since being recruited by a close friend of his uncle's just a year ago when he was at Oxford. It had been a very difficult decision to make and he knew he could not reveal it to any of his family or friends. Not even his beloved mama and papa.

Erik's father Boris Roskov had held his office in the Government for 15 years, and he had intricate knowledge of the workings of the Politburo and the entire Russian government. Ivan Roskov also held the rank of three star general in the Russian military, but he had not been active in the military since the old Soviet Union was, in effect, dismantled under the leadership of former Soviet leader, Mikhail Gorbachev. Had Ivan known the political changes that were going to take place in the Soviet Union during the 1980s he may have decided differently about sending his beloved son to England to be educated. It was the result of this decision that was responsible for his son Erik being a passenger in the black sedan on this deserted mountain road.

Chapter 2

Greta had been awakened abruptly by the telephone ringing on her night stand very early this morning. As she picked up the phone from its cradle and placed it to her ear and said with a very soft voice, "Hello this is Greta."

There was a momentary silence and then a very weak stuttering voice of a man who said, "Greta you don't have much time they're coming. Burn all the documents leave nothing that can be traced to the Wormwood project. Then do what you know you have to do. I am so sorry, but we all knew the risks." And then a click and the line was dead. Although she did not know who the voice was on the telephone that morning, she knew she had to act quickly and obey the command. Greta knew very well the risks that were involved when her and her husband Thomas accepted a position on the

Wormwood project. They both knew, along with all the other members of the project, if they were discovered before the project was ready to be executed, each of them could be imprisoned or even put to death. The old regime in Russia did not tolerate dissidents or even allow any opposition to their rule of tyranny.

Chapter 3

Otto Zorkov knew very well the sound of the military chopper, whirring in a low drone over his mountain cabin. He had heard it many times while he served in the prestigious Air Military Guard, of the Soviet Union's Northern Air Command, an elite air attack force. Not since he was wounded in an air campaign against the rebel held bunker in the mountains of Afghanistan and was sent home to retire after a three-month stay in the military hospital had he heard a military chopper of this class. Flying this close to his cabin, they usually flew in an air corridor some 30 kilometers east of his little isolated cabin. The roaring drone of the large primary props grew increasingly louder, and louder, former Colonel Otto Zorkov was curious to see this military chopper so close to his cabin. He set his small glass of vodka down on the coffee table in front of the settee, patted his large Irish setter, who was his only companion since he lost his dear wife three years ago, after a prolonged illness. He ambled toward the back door, as he reached for the knob to swing the door open he could not believe his ears. It was that all too familiar sound he had heard so many times during his campaign's when he was a member of the Military Guard in the Air Force, it was unmistakable. He heard, "Whoomp. Whoomp," then that shrill whistle, two missiles had just been launched. A deafening explosion and a blinding light followed soon after.

Chapter 4

Sid could see a small quaint mountain cabin at the bottom of the valley, just as the sedan topped the ridge. There was a wisp of smoke curling up from the chimney and he let his mind wander. He had often considered purchasing a small cabin somewhere in the mountains, where he could set in front of a crude stone fireplace and write his memoirs after he retired. After all he had much to write about, not only as a driver and companion of his boss for the past five years, but also many intriguing stories that he could tell about his experience of eight years he served as a member of the old Soviet Union's secret police the KGB. That was the best of times for Sid. All the undercover work and covert operations he was involved with. It was very exciting for a young man that grew up on the streets. That was when he first met Erik's father. He went to work as an undercover Intelligence Agent who reported directly to Boris Roskov. Then when Erik returned from England, they became friends and eventually led to his becoming the personal driver for Erik.

Sid heard a voice call from the rear of the sedan, which quickly brought him out of his dream state, "Yes Boss?"

"Pull the car over to the side of the road and stop." Without hesitation Sid steered the black sedan to the edge of the mountain road and stopped. The back door was opened and Erik said, "It looks like were about 2 kilometers from the cabin." As he got out of the sedan he raised a pair of binoculars to his eyes. "I want to see what we may be walking into before we are seen," said Erik in a halting voice. "Pull the car up into those trees so it can't be seen from the air, and you stay with the car." Erik slipped cautiously down toward the cabin with his shoulder holster undone and his pistol at the ready. He came up to the rear of the cabin and he did not see the green Volkswagen pull out of the driveway in the front of the cabin.

When Erik entered the cabin through the back door it was empty, but there was a computer burning in the fireplace along with a lot of paper files. He tried to retrieve them but it was too late they were too far burned. He wondered who tipped her off, that he was coming to apprehend her.

Chapter 5

Greta had just topped the hill, out of sight in her little Volkswagen when Erik stormed through the back door with his pistol in his hand and ready to fire. As she drove away she let all kinds of thoughts race through her mind. Did I leave any trace of the project behind? I think I burned everything, but I can't be sure. After all I didn't have much time. The mysterious voice on the phone alerted me early this morning and it is now 7:15. I had to hurry and I could have missed something. Should I have taken the cyanide pill as the man on the phone said? We all agreed that it should end that way for each of us if we were ever discovered before the project could be executed. I don't know if I did the right thing by taking the files on the computer disk with me. I felt I had to have more time to determine, if what we had agreed to do on the project was morally right. If it would accomplish the end of wars, and bring about world peace as we all had been told it would. If only my husband was here he would know what to do.

Greta had been grieving over her husband's disappearance. He had been missing now for six months, and she was nearly out of her mind with worry. She did not have the time or the will to attend the last two project meetings, and she was beginning to think that her husband's disappearance had something to do with the project. Her husband, Thomas, had raised several difficult and embarrassing questions at the last meeting they attended together in January.

The project leader, Colonel Ivan Chechnikov, said from the floor during that meeting, that he would answer any questions. Anyone who had questions concerning the project, in a private forum, but this was not the place for that. We heard no more until March, when Thomas received a voicemail inviting him to the project headquarters in Moscow for a meeting with Colonel Chechnikov. To answer the questions he raised at the meeting in January.

Since Greta had come down with a severe case of the flu, she thought it best to stay home. Thomas decided to attend the meeting alone. He packed an overnight bag and left the cabin in the mountains, east of Moscow where they lived, on March 15, and she had not heard from him since. The day after he left she received a phone call from the secretary of

Colonel Chichnikov, inquiring why her husband had chosen not to attend the meeting. If he was sick she would reschedule it for next week. Greta's heart leaped within her chest. She immediately knew something was wrong. Her husband was very diligent in letting his wife know his whereabouts at all times. Greta picked up the phone to call the police, but she hesitated, and placed it back in the cradle. Otto, who was her and her husband's friend, lived only two kilometers north of her cabin. He was always willing to help them when they needed help. Otto was the reason they had moved out of the apartment in the city to their cabin in the mountains. He had heard about this cabin being empty after an elderly man who lived there had died. He told her husband about it and he made some inquiries to the elderly man's family, and was able to purchase the cabin.

Otto had said, "It's so beautiful and quiet and peaceful out here, and I am only two kilometers north if you ever need anything." He had been such a good friend so Greta decided to enlist his help in locating her missing husband after he had failed to return home from the meeting. Otto was a Colonel in the military and he knew a lot of people in government.

Greta slipped on her coat and gloves wrapped a wool scarf around her neck, she knew that the mountain air was unusually cool even in March. Then she climbed into her green Volkswagen and headed back up the mountain road. She drove about three kilometers where the road turned into a fork and made a hard left turn down the other leg of the fork towards Otto's cabin. Now she would have to drive three kilometers back even though his cabin was only two kilometers across from her cabin, separated only by a small rocky ridge that made both of their cabins impossible to be seen from the other. She arrived at Otto's to find him outside with his dog. Greta pulled her green Volkswagen into the drive behind Otto's car, turned off the engine and got out. Precious, Otto's big dog ran to meet her with Otto right behind, "Come in Greta. Good to see you. Where's Thomas?" Greta told Otto what had happened as she began to cry, she knew something terrible had happened to her husband. "There, there Greta. I'll find Thomas he's probably broke down somewhere on the road to the city. You stay here with Precious and have some hot coffee. I just made it. I'll be back with Thomas before dark."

Greta sat down on the settee to have a cup of coffee, and to wait for Otto to return. He could easily run the whole route that Thomas would have taken into the city and be back in a couple of hours. Otto returned home after two and a half hours. He said to Greta, "I couldn't find any trace of Thomas or his car. Don't worry, I will go into the city tomorrow and make some inquiries. I'm sure someone must've seen him. I'll check with all the hospitals as well. Perhaps he had an accident and is unable to contact you. Don't worry we will find Thomas." Greta drove back to her cabin to await word from Otto and to be there in case Thomas called.

That was six months ago, since then a lot had happened. Otto had checked in all the local hospitals, inquired in all the government offices in the Kremlin, where Thomas might have had business, checked all the local garages and towing services to see if anyone had seen his car, but he turned up nothing. It was as though Thomas Burkov had just disappeared.

Sometime in August, after he had given up the search for Thomas, Otto received a strange e-mail message that read, "Stop searching and inquiring about the disappearance of T. Burkov. Continued inquiries will endanger the life of his wife Greta, signed a friend." Otto didn't know if he should tell Greta about the e-mail message or not. It could just be a prank, after all a lot of people knew Thomas was missing. He decided not to tell her, and let her get on with her life without Thomas. Since Thomas's disappearance, Greta and Otto had been spending a lot of time together. Nothing had happened untoward, but Greta was a delightful woman and pleasant to look at. With her long auburn hair that cascaded like a soft stream of water down around her shoulders, her beautiful green eyes, and near perfect face. She was of slight build, but very well proportioned from her legs all the way up to her head on her 5'7" frame. It'd been over three years since he had even been remotely interested in another woman, but Greta was a beautiful woman whom he enjoyed spending time with.

Otto's mind went back to the wonderful times he and his wife shared together for 14 years. He was in the military when they met and fell in love. They were married shortly after they met and lived on military bases the rest of their married life. Otto was a colonel in the military so it was not a hard life for them. They enjoyed traveling to many European countries and seeing the sights together. Otto had nearly lost his mind when his wife became suddenly sick while he was in Afghanistan and died in less than two weeks.

The death certificate ruled the death to be a brain tumor. It had been three long years, but this was not the time to let Greta know about his feelings toward her. Thomas was not dead he was only missing, and he was a dear friend. Otto decided he would continue to poke around quietly while he was at his office. Even after he retired from the air military guard, due to his injuries, he was given an office in the Kremlin. Assigned to the International Space Station Project where he was responsible for reviewing procedures and government classified documents. To make sure no top-secret documents slipped through into the public arena. He was useful since he had top-secret clearance from his position in the Soviet military.

One day in September when Otto was reviewing some classified files from a computer disk that was dropped off in his office by mistake by a courier from the department in Kremlin that was responsible for the military oversight on the International Space Station Project. His curiosity was aroused when he read the routing label attached to the documents envelope containing the disk stamped top secret. He thought it seemed odd since all documents for review on the International Space Station were all stamped classified. Only military documents were stamped top-secret. As he placed the disk into his computer and opened the window on his viewing screen he saw the file was prompting for the password for the highest level of military intelligence top-secret clearance. That was the highest clearance in the military, why was it on a file from the department overseeing the International Space Station? All of that oversight was in the pervue of the civilian planning department, and their group of contractors. Otto was the more curious when he typed in his high clearance password and saw a name he was unfamiliar with, Colonel Ivan Chechnikov.

He was sure he knew all the military personnel that would have this high clearance access, so who is this Colonel Chechnikov? As he scrolled down the file, he noticed it contained a lot of dates with check marks after them, but then he recognized the last entry in the short list of names. It was the name of the Russian cosmonaut that was scheduled to be lifted into orbit next week, Sergeis Kerikalev. To take a three month tour of duty on the International Space Station, to relieve an American astronaut who had been there three months. Next to his name was written comrade do not forget to deliver the package Project Wormwood depends on you. It was signed Colonel I. Chechnikov. Although Otto knew nothing of Project Wormwood, he would have just closed the file and placed the envelope with the disk in the re-route mail slot to forward it to its rightful recipient, but he caught a glimpse of a name as he was scrolling that got his attention. Mr. and Mrs. Thomas Burkov.

Chapter 6

Otto was lying on a small rocky ledge at the back of his cabin where he had landed when the missiles obliterated his cabin. There was a drop-off at the rear of his cabin out from the porch about 20 feet and then there was a rocky ledge jutting out from the side of the face of the cliff, which formed the table down about 6 feet from the top of the cliff. This is where Otto was now lying, nearly buried with the debris from the cabin. Every bone and muscle in his body ached, but he was alive. When he had heard the missiles being launched he acted on instinct and dove off the porch to land on the ground about six feet out in a tuck position. Then rolled head over heels the remaining 12 feet or so until he dropped down onto the table rock where he was now lying. Otto heard a male voice that seemed to be talking to someone on a two-way radio. He remained very still and quiet the man said, "There's nothing left but the foundation and kindling scattered all over the site where the cabin stood. You won't have to worry about Mrs. Burkov anymore. Her remains are scattered all over the mountain valley. The chopper made a direct hit with both missiles."

"I don't see any sign of the general's son or his driver. The sedan they were driving is no where in site. They must have taken a wrong turn and got lost and never made it to the cabin. We are returning to base now mission accomplished."

Mrs. Burkov, thought Otto as he pulled himself out from under the debris. Why would anyone think Greta was here? Her cabin is two kilometer further south and who would want Greta killed? Then it dawned on him, the chopper hit the wrong target.

Otto lay on the stone table for nearly 2 hours thinking and trying to convince his body to start working again. As he lay there thinking, he remembered the computer disk that he had reviewed in his office, and the names of Thomas and Greta Burkov with others could this be connected somehow? And what is this Project Wormwood that the unknown Colonel Chechnikov was referring to?

Otto knew he had a day or two before anyone realized they had hit the wrong target. This was Monday, so he would file an official report to his commander on Wednesday, and act as though he was out of town since Sunday, when he returned he found his cabin in splinters. He would then ask if some military training maneuver had gone awry and somehow destroyed his cabin with a misdirected missile. Then he would file a report to receive compensation for the damage done and watch and see who would bear the responsibility.

Otto knew he had to contact Greta and let her know she was in danger, but just as he was climbing up to the top of the cliff he heard a woman screaming his name. He saw Greta running toward him. Greta helped him pull himself up out of his hiding place. Then she put both her arms around him and held on tight all the time sobbing incessantly.

Otto told Greta what happened and what he over heard them saying about her. Greta became visibly shaken and for the first time she knew her life was in danger. It was somehow related to her and Thomas working on the Wormwood Project. Then she began to sob and said, "I believe they killed Thomas but why?" Otto insisted that she tell him all she knew about this project. At first Greta was hesitant but then she believed she could trust him and told him all she knew. As it turned out she knew very little. The details of the project were never revealed to her or the other members. Colonel Chechnikov said it was to protect us and our families. She and the other members were given assignments mostly paperwork, invoices to check, schedules and appointments to make. They also were to solicit funds from people they knew by telling them that when the project was executed it would bring about world peace. They were also told that if they were discovered and the project was revealed by the old Soviet hierarchy, they would be tried as dissidents and either imprisoned or executed as traitors to the state.

Chapter 7

As the large military transport truck pulled away from the dock at the secluded warehouse in the mountains and through the heavily guarded security gate, it was raining hard and a fog had drifted in over the mountain road. The driver of the truck could hardly see the road as it snaked down the mountain. He had traveled this route many times before, but not in heavy fog. He knew there were steep sharp curves all along the route but he also knew he had to make it to the warehouse at the International Space Station complex before daylight. He had been instructed that he could not enter the complex after daylight, after the guards had changed shifts.

The driver said to the man sitting in the passenger seat of the truck, "Help me watch for those sharp turns. We don't want to drive off of this mountain."

The man sitting next to him wearing a military uniform shook his head in acknowledgement. “Look out! There's a sharp turn dead ahead.” The driver applied the brakes to the big deuce truck, but it was too late. He could not slow the truck down enough to make that turn. The truck turned abruptly and it was too much. The cargo shifted and the truck rolled over on its side. Neither the driver nor his passenger was injured, but neither of them knew what to do now. Then the driver looked at his bill of lading to see if there was a phone number to call in case of an emergency. There was, so he called the number on his cell phone. He reported to the man who answered the phone at the other end about the accident. He was told to stay with the truck and he would send a wrecker out. It was well after daylight when the wrecker arrived at the scene. By then the driver had set out traffic cones to direct traffic, going into the city, around the accident scene.

It was just by accident that Bill Forney, a British reporter on a local television talk show, was passing by on his way into the city. He stopped and began taking a series of pictures of the truck and its cargo. He was especially interested in the crates of material scattered on the side of the road that had the signs for radioactive material painted on them. Bill began to interview the driver and take pictures of his manifest when a big black sedan arrived. The doors swung open and four men in military uniforms jumped out waving their hands in the air to clear the area of bystanders. They backed up their gestures with the automatic rifles each of them were carrying. Then a large man with a thick gray mustache got out of the sedan, he was wearing a Russian Officers military uniform. He walked directly over to the over turned truck and began talking to the driver and his passenger. Bill knew it was time for him to leave the premises before his camera and his interview pad was confiscated. He had enough pictures and an interview with the driver to open his morning TV show with a very interesting topic.

"Welcome to the Bill Forney morning show." the announcer said as Bill took his seat behind the desk.

"Good morning friends," Bill said "We have a very interesting show today. We will go to the phones and take all your calls after we run some film that we made this morning. This morning as I was coming into the studio I came upon an accident on a mountain road that I drive each day. There was a large truck turned over on its side, it appeared to have failed to negotiate a sharp turn in the road due to the heavy fog last night. No one was injured. What makes this an unusual topic for discussion is the contents of the cargo the truck was carrying. Look at these pictures." As the pictures Bill had taken at the scene of the accident were being displayed on the television screen, "And you tell me if there isn't something very interesting about the crates of cargo this truck was carrying. See those radioactive material signs painted on the crates, but you don't see any of the same signs anywhere on the truck, which is required by law. And where were they being transported from? There are no nuclear facilities up in these mountains. And where were the military guards which are required by law for any radioactive material being transported by truck? There was one lone military personnel riding inside the truck with the driver. If this is not odd enough listen to this, after I was there about an hour, a black unmarked sedan arrived on the scene carrying four heavily armed military personnel and a Full Bird Colonel. I have pictures of them too, but you will have to tune in tomorrow morning to see them."

Chapter 8

Otto had a small efficiency apartment in the city where he stayed during the extreme winter months, rather than trying to get to and from his office on those treacherous mountain roads when they were covered with snow and ice. He insisted that Greta stay there with him. She could sleep in the bed and he would sleep on the couch. Greta agreed to stay at least till Otto could find out who tried to kill her and why she would be a threat to anyone. They didn't feel it was safe to return to Greta's cabin and get any clothes, but when she left the cabin she knew she probably would not be coming back for some time, so she packed a few things she thought she would need.

Otto returned to his office on Wednesday morning and went straight to his commander's office and told him about his cabin. At first his commander thought Otto was joking, but then he realized he was very serious. He instructed Otto as to the correct forms to file for compensation as he became emotionally shaken at the thought Otto could have been inside his cabin when the missile hit. He then picked up the phone and called the Chief of Security Operations and said, "My office at once." Otto left the office as the Chief of Security entered.

"You incompetent fool! Your pilot did not get rid of Mrs. Burkov as you reported. Instead he hit the wrong target. It's no wonder that there was no sign of the general's son or the sedan they were at the right cabin and probably have Mrs. Burkov hidden away in a safe house being debriefed on the Wormwood project. Colonel Chechnikov is going to be furious."

Chapter 9

Erik was sitting in his office adjacent to his father's office on Wednesday morning when the door opened and Otto burst in all excited. “Did you hear what happened to my cabin over the weekend?”

“No, what happened?” Eric asked.

“The military was conducting an exercise in the mountains. One of their attack helicopters shot a misdirected missile and hit my cabin and completely destroyed it.”

“Was anybody hurt?” Erik said.

“No!” Otto exclaimed, “No one was there. I was lucky I was out of town all weekend on personal business and didn't return home until Monday morning.”

Erik remembered what Sid had said as he was getting into the sedan near the Burkov cabin, about hearing an explosion and feeling the ground move. It wasn't blasting as he thought it was. It was a missile hitting Otto's cabin, just two kilometers north of where he was.

"Otto," Erik said, "I am so glad you're all right and I will personally have my office conduct an investigation to find out who's responsible for this. You're a very special friend to me, you and your lovely wife before she died."

"Erik, while I'm thinking of it I would like to ask a question about a colonel in the Russian military. A man by the name of Ivan Chechnikov do you know him?"

"I never heard the name before." Erik said, "Is he someone I should know?"

"I'm not sure, the name just came up in a conversation and I thought I knew all our military officers, but I've not heard of him." Otto wasn't comfortable enough to discuss the information he saw on the computer disk with his friend just yet.

"I'll see what I can find out about him in the course of our investigation and if I turn up anything or talk to anyone who knows him, I'll let you know."

Only one year after he returned to Russia from England Erik's beloved mother had succumbed to the cancer and died. He was so glad he was able to be with her the last year she lived. During that year he hardly ever left her side. It was difficult seeing his mother suffer with that dreadful disease. First she had to endure the chemotherapy and then the radiation treatments, but it was too late when she was diagnosed. The cancer had already spread to her vital organs and was in the worst stages of development.

When his mother died Erik went into a deep depression. His father tried to console him by taking a three-month leave from his office. He and Erik went into the mountains in Saint Petersburg where the family owned a cabin. They could hunt, fish and just get to know each other for they had been apart for eight long years.

The days became shorter and shorter while Erik and his father spent each day either hunting bear and deer or fishing in their favorite trout streams. They knew they would soon have to return to the city and his father would have to return to his office. The last week they were in the mountains Erik's father talked more and more to his son about what he was going to do as a vocation. Erik had a degree in political science that he received from Oxford University. He had thought he would like to apply for some government position, probably something in the military intelligence division.

Erik confided to his father that he was interested in doing military investigative work. His father was happy to hear that and offered him a position on his personal staff. He would head the Department of the Military Intelligence Bureau and report directly to him. Since the KGB covert intelligence agency had been dismantled, the military had very few effective intelligence agents left in the bureau. Erik accepted his father's offer knowing he would have an office adjacent to his father's and have full access to all military intelligence files. He had not told his Father that he was a British Intelligence Agent, and that his assignment was to uncover all the information he could on the mysterious Project Wormwood.

Erik thought it was ironic that he was sent to England to be educated and while at Oxford University he was solicited by the British intelligence to become an MI5 agent. Which he eventually accepted, and now he would have free access to all the military intelligence files of the whole former Soviet Union. But he still could not reveal his identity to his beloved father that he was a spy.

The British had received an important piece of information on a back channel source a year before Erik returned to Russia concerning a project called Wormwood. The information they received indicated this project was being conducted by a shadow military force in Russia and it could adversely affect the whole world economy if it was allowed to be implemented. They did not have any real details of what the project involved, but they did have unconfirmed information from their back channel source before it ended, that somehow the International Space Station was involved in the project. It was because of this information that there was much anxiety at the British intelligence high command. A dozen of their field agents were given a special assignment to try and recruit a high-ranking or a very influential Russian, preferably military, that they could train and assign to investigate inside Russia. So that they could either confirm or deny if the information was true or just a rumor being spread. And if Project Wormwood was true they would be directed to find out all the information they could about it, including the persons in the shadow military group. It took eight months of intense training and development for the British high command to be comfortable enough with Erik to reveal to him his primary assignment.

Chapter 10

Bill Forney met Erik when they were at Oxford University when he was attending classes in journalism. One day his professor said they were going to have a guest lecturer who was from a prominent Soviet military family in Russia. The professor knew this would peak Bill's interest since he was also studying the Russian language. Bill had confided in his professor that he was interested in pursuing a journalism career in a foreign country, either Russia or the United States. When Erik was introduced to the class, Bill was surprised to see such a young man who was barely out of his teens. He expected someone much older. He was captivated by this young Russian and they became very close friends.

Bill left Oxford a short time before Erik, but Erik assured his close friend that when he returned to Russia he would surely get in touch with him. Bill flew to Moscow two weeks after he left Oxford. He had applied to this new TV station that was looking for a multilingual journalist to do field investigative work and remote broadcasting. Since he applied on the internet they summoned him to Moscow for an interview. Bill got the job and started work immediately, he loved this kind of journalism. He was given complete control of his investigations and the broadcasting of the story. The TV station manager was so pleased with his work he gave him a permanent slot on the evening broadcast. Bill Forney soon became a familiar name to all the Russian households.

After only six months of investigative reporting from the field, the station manager offered Bill an anchor position on the evening news. Bill accepted it and soon after that he had his own morning TV talk show. In which he was featured in exposé style of investigative reporting.

Bill was sitting in his office going over some documents when his secretary said on her intercom, “There's a gentleman here who wishes to speak with you, but he won't tell me his name. He just said to tell you to remember Oxford.” Bill sat for a minute thinking back to Oxford and who could this be?

“Erik?” Bill said as he opened his office door into the outer office, “Is that you?” Bill stood looking into the face of this ruggedly handsome redhead who was his old friend, whom he had not seen or heard from in nearly eight months. "How long have you been back in Russia? Come in to the office and sit down we have a lot of catching up to do." Looking at his secretary he said, "Hold all my calls. I'm not seeing anyone or taking any calls the remainder of the day."

Erik told his old friend about his dear mother and how she was dying of cancer. Bill said, "I'm so sorry old friend is there anything I can do to help?"

"No Bill, it's too late she only has a short time left."

Bill told Erik how he'd worked his way up the ladder at the station in such a short time. "It has been a phenomenal rise and now I have my own morning TV talk show. Hey! I'll have you on some time as a guest. You just tell me when you're free and I'll have my secretary book you."

It had been eight years since Erik first appeared in Bill's office at the television station. In those eight years they had become so close they were nearly inseparable. Bill was just the kind of a friend Erik needed to get over his dear mother's death. They attended nearly every social function together. Erik was usually without a lady friend, but Bill on the other hand was quite the ladies man. Even though he was happily married, he and his wife did not travel in the same circles. She was too busy raising their daughter to attend all the social functions with her husband Bill. Just about two years ago, Bill and Erik were at some military social gathering that Erik's father was hosting and they met Colonel Otto Zorkov who was a pleasant man. Who had just recently lost his wife to a prolonged illness. Erik could empathize with him because of his mother's death and the three of them became fast friends.

Bill was in and out of General Roskov's office complex so often that Erik's father, General Boris Roskov jokingly said, “Erik don't let that journalist into our file cabinet. He will dig out every skeleton the KGB ever buried.” Then he gave a friendly laugh.

General Boris Roskov was this jovial and friendly man who had a laugh that could be heard from a hundred yards away. He had eyes so full of affection and set so deeply in his forehead that his face looked as if it had been sculptured out of clay by a Michael Angelo or another great artist. He was the Father of Erik Roskov and the husband of his beloved Anna who was taken from him by a cancerous tumor that proved to be inoperable. He was a Soviet Union military hero who had led his forces through many decisive campaigns. Not the least of which was the Afghanistan invasion by the old Soviet Union government forces. It was during that campaign that General Roskov was promoted to the high rank of three star general which he continues to hold. He, Erik, and Anna were an inseparable family, who were loved and respected by all the Soviet people. When Anna died the new Russian Government insisted on a State funeral. It was as if the mother of the country had died.

It nearly broke the general's heart when he made the decision to send his twelve year old son to England to live with Anna's Brother Jerrod. Boris believed it was the right decision, because He and Anna were constantly traveling for the military. When Erik reached the age of twelve, he wanted his son to have the finest education possible. It nearly broke Anna's heart, but she knew it was the right decision also. After all he would be living with her brother, and his father could visit him often when he traveled to England on state business.

General Roskov loved Erik's friend Bill Forney like a second son and often took him and his beautiful wife and daughter with him and Erik to their family cabin in the mountains of Saint. Petersburg, where they vacationed by hunting and fishing. Bill's wife often said jokingly, "The only reason they include me is so they will have someone to clean and cook the game they catch and clean up after them."

It had been a long journey for General Roskov. He began his career in the military by attending a government run school for orphans. The old Soviet Union did not call them orphans because they would never admit to the people that, under the communist controlled state there could ever be anything but perfection in a controlled society.

His mother died when he was just an infant. Then his father took him and tried to raise him in his small apartment with his live in girl friend whom he never married. He and his girlfriend drank vodka at all hours of the day and night and when they were drunk they would fight till one of them passed out in a drunken stupor. Then when they awoke the next day it would begin all over again. Mary, his father's girlfriend received a small allotment from the government, because of her husband's death while serving in the military. His father was a mechanic but he seldom worked because he drank so much. With both of their incomes Mary and his father barely made enough to buy a little bread and beans and a little milk for Boris to live on. All the rest was used to buy vodka.

Then one day when Boris was only six years old both his Father and Mary were found dead in the apartment. They had drank so much vodka that their hearts just stopped. The Postman found them and took Boris and turned him over to the state run school. From the very first day at school Boris fit in with all the other students and enjoyed being there. He excelled in everything he did and was soon a special student to all his teachers. The first four hours of the day were devoted to academics and then for four hours, after they were served a little lunch, they were required to attend the military training side of the school. Boris found that he excelled even more in the military training. So much so that at the age of ten he was placed in a special state run military training school where he remained until he was fifteen. Then he was placed in the Soviet Army to serve his country.

Because of his disciplined nature he rose in rank rapidly and became a Soviet hero who fought in many campaigns. When he was a young lieutenant barley twenty years old, he met and fell deeply in love with Anna, Erik's mother. They were married soon after they met and nine months later Erik was born. For the next eight years Boris and his young family traveled all over the Soviet Union and Europe. Boris rose to the rank of general and then two years later he was promoted to the rank of three star general. Erik was ten and had to be left at home with a favorite aunt to attend school while his mother accompanied Boris.

Chapter 11

Bill was working late at the station when he got a phone call. The man on the other end of the line, "If you meet me down by the docks at pier 33 tonight at 11:30, I'll give you some information on the radioactive material piece you did on the show today. This information exposes a secret shadow military project."

Bill anxiously said, "I will be there, but I will want to tape our interview."

The caller calmly spoke, "That will be okay, if I don't have to reveal my name." Bill agreed.

It was 9:30 now, so he had two hours. He would grab a bite to eat at the diner and then head on down to the pier and wait. Bill arrived at the pier around 10:45. He looked around, but stayed inside his car with it running. He was not naïve. He had been doing these kinds of meetings for a long time, and he was always prepared for any emergency. It was true Bill had a nose for news, but he also had a sixth sense for danger. It was 11:15 when the black sedan came into view, driving slowly down the docks toward pier 33 with its lights out. Bill could make out the silhouette in the moonlight. The closer he got to Bill's car the more uneasy Bill felt, something was wrong. Bill had purposely driven down early so he could plan a route of escape, if it became necessary. He had his car pointed in the direction that he would escape any danger coming up behind him, and there was no way into the docks from in front of him. If he had to bolt he could cut off a car behind him, and cut through the alleys in between the dock buildings. If he kept his lights out, and just drove by moonlight, he could give the slip to any car that might be chasing him. As the sedan moved closer to Bill's car he became more uneasy. The sedan stopped about 20 yards behind his car and he saw the passenger-side door open. He couldn't see a person because they had disengaged the interior light. Bill sat there waiting as the lone figure strode slowly toward his car. Then it happened, both back doors of the sedan opened and two more men got out. Bill could clearly see by their silhouettes that both of them were carrying what looked like automatic rifles. The first man was now about ten feet from Bill's car. He could see that he too was carrying a pistol in his hand.

Bill hit the accelerator hard and the car bolted forward. It surprised all three men and they began running back toward the sedan. Bill turned sharply down the first alley, drove rapidly to the next turn, and just as he made that turn he could see the sedan was pursuing him. He was confident he could lose them in the maze of alleyways and get back onto the road and into the mainstream of traffic without being caught.

Bill didn't return to his house in the mountains. He was afraid they would be watching for him on the narrow mountain roads. He knew they would be watching his office, so he drove around about two hours. Then Bill called his old friend Erik. "Erik, I need somewhere to stay tonight. Have you got company?"

"No, I'm alone Bill. What is this all about?" Erik asked.

"I'll explain when I get there, but right now I believe my life is in danger. Someone is trying to kill me."

"Come on over Bill." Erik said, "I'm up now. I'll put on a pot of coffee, it sounds like this is going to be a long night."

When Bill arrived at Erik's it was well past midnight. Erik was waiting up for his old friend with a fresh pot of coffee and some sandwiches he had fixed after Bill called. "Come in and sit down Bill," Erik said, "and have a cup of hot coffee, and I made some sandwiches. It looks like we have a great deal to talk about."

After Bill calmed down a little he began to tell Erik about the incident that happened tonight. He also told him about the wreck in the mountains, the pictures and interview he took, and the military Colonel at the site with his armed guards. “It sounds like you have stumbled onto something big Bill.” Erik said, “I think whoever that Colonel is, he didn't like his picture being taken. You say that the truck driver’s cargo manifest showed the delivery of that radioactive material to be going to the International Space Station complex?”

“That's right Erik.” Bill said.

“But why there? And where was he coming from?” Erik said.

“The driver wouldn't tell me anything, and the passenger in the military uniform kept trying to get rid of me. He seemed embarrassed about me being there.”

It was daylight when Erik finally said to his friend Bill, “You look like you can use some sleep. You stay here and go to bed. Don't leave here until I get back from my office, and don't contact anyone either. I'll be home around five o'clock and I will pick up some dinner for us on the way home.”

Erik arrived at his office at the usual time and said good morning to the receptionist. He went to his office and went straight to his desk. Picking up the phone he tapped in a number. “Good morning Otto, this is Erik. Are you going to be very busy today?”

"No not really. Why?" Otto said.

"I would like for you to stop by my office sometime today for a talk."

"What's it about?" Otto said.

"I'll explain when you get here. Give yourself about two hours for the meeting."

"I'll be there right after lunch." Otto said and hung up the phone. Erik then walked across the hall, to his father's office. General Boris Roskov, Erik's father, was not in his office. Erik told the receptionist he would wait in his father's office until he arrived. The receptionist smiled and acknowledged what Erik said.

Chapter 12

Greta was so nervous ever since she moved into Otto's apartment. She was afraid to go out in public, and because she had so much time to think about all that had happened she found herself crying quite often. Otto was such a sweet generous man. He would bring her a hot lunch each day, and they would sit and talk until it was time for Otto to return to his office. She had loaded the computer discs, she had brought from her cabin, onto Otto's computer, and watched them over and over to try and see if there was anything on them that would be a threat to anyone. Her husband Thomas did most of the computer programming for the project, but she did occasionally get involved herself. A long list of donors they had contacted and other members of their tier group. Then there was a list of dates of meetings that they had set up, and a short list of names which she was not familiar with, but her husband probably knew who they were. After each of these names there was a letter or a symbol. Chechnikov, she knew, there was a symbol of an eagle after his name. Two other names had a "C" after them, and there were three names with stars after them. Two names had a "M" after their's.

Greta heard Otto's car drive up, was it lunch time already? It was always the best part of the day. When she an Otto sat together and just talked at lunchtime. "Greta," Otto said as he opened the door of the apartment. "I have a nice hot lunch for you. We're having shrimp and scallops today with a salad and that special pudding you like so well." Greta rushed toward Otto and put her arms around him and greeted him with a kiss on the cheek. She had not yet been intimate with Otto, but she was having a difficult time suppressing her natural urges.

Greta and Otto sat down and ate their lunch together. Then Otto said he was getting worried about leaving Greta at the apartment while he was at his office all day. He knew if someone wanted her dead, and they had the military at their disposal, they would surely be able to find her eventually. Otto had been coming home late at night because he didn't trust himself being in the apartment with Greta until after she retired to the bedroom. Otto was beginning to have strong feelings for her. And with the weekend coming he knew that he was going to be with her much longer than he needed to be.

Otto told Greta that he was having a meeting after lunch with a friend of his. While he is there he would ask his friend if he could use his cabin in the mountains of Saint Petersburg, to seclude Greta away and out of danger for a while. Just until he could find out why anyone wanted to kill her. He assured Greta that this friend could be trusted, and because he was in the military intelligence he could help Otto in his investigation of who is trying to kill her. Greta agreed to go if it could be arranged.

Chapter 13

At 1 o'clock Otto was buzzed into Erik's office by his secretary. "Come in Otto and have a seat, I didn't mean to sound mysterious on the phone this morning, but I thought it best we discussed in private what I'm about to ask you to do. Otto," Erik said, "since you review all the documents, invoices, and other paperwork for the International Space Station Project, I need your help." Then Erik told Otto about their friend Bill Forney nearly being killed last night, and all the information that led up to the incident. Including the wreck in the mountains, the cargo manifest, the mysterious Colonel, and the television show. "Otto," Erik said, "I would like for you to see if you can find out anything that the military or the government is doing over there at the International Space Station Agency that is being done undercover, and if exposed would be a threat to anyone and who?" Then Otto told his friend about the computer disk he had seen and the name of this Colonel Chechnikov, and this Wormwood Project that he didn't know anything about. They wondered if this could be the mysterious colonel Bill photographed at the scene of the overturned truck in the mountains.

Then Otto confided in his friend about Greta, and the military helicopter that launched the missiles into his cabin. "That was not an accident." as Otto had told his friend when it happened. "They hit the wrong target. They were really sent to kill Greta by blowing up her cabin. Greta's cabin is just two kilometers further south from mine right in line. The only thing that separates it is a rocky ridge, which apparently the helicopter pilot couldn't see over and hit the wrong cabin." Then Otto asked Erik if he could possibly allow Greta to stay secluded in his cabin in the mountains of Saint Petersburg for a while, until he was able to sort all this out to keep her safe. Erik agreed and drew Otto a map of the location and how to get there.

It was like pieces of a puzzle, which was all starting to come together now. Erik could not reveal to his friend Otto that he was a spy for the British Intelligence Agency. Erik could not tell Otto that he was sent to take her into custody and send her to England for questing. He knew he was now involved in something that was a threat to someone high in the government or the military, or perhaps both. And he also knew it involved the International Space Station or the agency in some way. His investigation was leading him to the mysterious Project Wormwood that he was assigned to find out about from his handlers England.

Erik sent an encrypted message by e-mail to Mr. O'Donnell in England. That was the code name he was to contact inside the agency. It read, “Received new and confirmed information concerning assignment, need to know identity of source of original information. If you can supply please do so. Need to contact original source in Russia for help in investigation. Assignment becoming very dangerous.

Chapter 14

Otto drove Greta to Erik's family cabin in the mountains of Saint Petersburg. It was a pleasurable trip and Greta seemed a little more relaxed. “Otto,” Greta said, “I know you have done all you can to help find Thomas. At least to find out what happened to him, and I want you to know how much I deeply appreciate it.”

When they arrived at the cabin it was dark, and they would never have been able to find it had Erik not drawn a very detailed map. It was very secluded in the mountains. Otto unloaded Greta’s things from the van, along with a sufficient supply of groceries that they had stopped on the way and bought. After everything was put away Greta said, “Otto, you're not driving back tonight? You're going to stay here with me?” Otto agreed since it was so late, and these mountain roads could be very dangerous after dark if you are unfamiliar with the area.

The cabin had one small bedroom, and there was a daybed in the main room. It also had a large stone fireplace with plenty of cut wood stacked just outside for the chilly nights. There was no inside plumbing, and the lieu was outside in back of the cabin.

Greta busied herself making some sandwiches while Otto built up a warm fire in the fireplace, and hung an old-fashioned coffeepot over the fire, full of real coffee beans that he had ground by hand on an old-fashioned coffee grinder he found at the cabin. The cabin did have electricity, but everything else was primitive. Greta would have to draw water from a nearby stream.

Greta walked over to the fireplace where Otto was sitting on the floor, on a bearskin rug, and sat down beside him. She put her arm around his neck and drew his head toward her to kiss him. They kissed for what seemed like a very long time to Otto. Then Greta said, "Otto you're sweet man. I think I have fallen in love with you, but it is still too early to allow me to express it. I need a little more time to find out what happened to Thomas."

"I feel the same for you," Otto said, "but you're right. Thomas was or is my friend, and until I know if he is dead or alive, my feelings for you cannot be expressed."

Otto kissed Greta goodbye the next morning and left for Moscow. Greta had a cell phone and though the area was isolated, it had a cell phone tower just down the road. She could call and talk to Otto each day because all of these cabins were owned by the Russian elite. The government had installed cell phone service, electricity, and satellite television in the whole area. Greta would have some of the comforts of home.

Chapter 15

Otto had been watching in the mail room for another mail pouch containing a computer disk, from the same source as the first one he received by mistake. Then, after about two weeks since he took Greta to Erik's cabin, another mail pouch with a computer disk came to the mailroom. Otto took it from the mailroom and took it to his office. He excitedly opened it being very careful not to damage the pouch, so he could replace the disk in it after he ran it. This disc had similar information on it that the first one contained, but after the names of Mr. and Mrs. Thomas Burkov was, "unknown and in-flight." It also contained several lists of names that were separated into different tier groups.

The Burkov's were listed in two different tiers. Thomas was in tier group four, while Greta was listed in tier group five. The name of the cosmonauts that were currently on the space station was listed in tier group number three. There were other unfamiliar names in tier group number two, alongside Col. Chechnikov. Then in tier group number one there was two names listed but they had been blacked out and Otto couldn't read them. Beside each tier group there was a list of responsibilities or job-related duties. Tier group number five's duties were, invoicing, scheduling, holding meetings with potential donors, and various other low-key duties. Beside tier group number four was listed, personal contact with high-profile donors, computer programming, and holding public meetings to raise public awareness on issues concerning, global warming, conflicts in the middle east, depleting of earth's energy supply, overuse of earth's energy between have and have not nations, and the disarmament of the nuclear warheads in Russia and The United States. Beside tier group number three was listed deliver the project packages, assembling the Project Wormwood, and implementing the project, at the command of tier group number one. Beside tier group number two was listed all military oversight of the space station, liaison between all tier groups below to tier group number one in which there were no responsibilities and the two names were blacked out.

Otto scrolled down through all the information on the disk until he found a list of dates with remarks after each one of them. It was now in the month of October, and the remarks after the dates listed in the month of June and the month of September were cosmonaut delivered second package, and cosmonaut delivered third package safely. Otto knew that these dates coincided with the subsequent launches of the cosmonauts to the International Space Station. The remarks after the December date, when the next scheduled launch was due to take place were, send two remaining packages, and begin the assembly of the project. Our schedule has been moved up due to circumstances beyond the control of tier group number two. Otto didn't know for sure what this information was telling him, so he copied the disk, with the intention of showing it to Erik and Greta. And then he repackaged the disk very carefully in the same mail pouch, and returned it to the mailroom. He could not determine who the intended recipient was, because under the words stamped top-secret there was a barcode. He believed the barcode identified the recipient.

Chapter 16

Erik received an e-mail message from the agency in England. It was an encrypted code, so it had to be deciphered. It read, the original source of the information on wormwood project, is Thomas Burkov, a field agent, he has not made contact with agency nor have we been able to contact him since the end of March last year. Trust this information will aid in your investigation. Good luck, Signed O'Donnell. Erik told his friend Otto he had to leave town on some business, and he would be back in his office in about three days.

Chapter 17

Bill Forney was now back at the television station doing his morning talk show, but only after he decided not to follow up on the last show, which he said he would show the photos of the mysterious colonel at the accident site. He thought that was probably why he received the unsigned e-mail message saying, "You have made an intelligent decision, you had better stick with it."

Bill was still an investigative reporter, and he knew there was an interesting story connected with that radioactive material. He would have to get to the bottom of it, even if it meant endangering his own life.

Chapter 18

Erik took a commercial flight to Saint Petersburg, and stayed overnight in the Pravda hotel. Sid, his driver, drove down in the sedan, and met him the next morning at the hotel. As they drove out to Erik's cabin, Erik was unusually quiet. Sid knew he should not disturb him by asking a lot of questions. Sid knew the route to the cabin. For in the five years that he had worked for Erik, he had come here with him and his father, to hunt and fish many times. The general had used this cabin as a safe house a few times when Sid worked for him as well.

It seemed rather strange to Sid, when they were about one kilometer from the cabin, and Erik told him to pull off the road and park the sedan. Erik got out of the sedan, checked to make sure he had his pistol, and made sure it was loaded. Sid said, “Trouble boss?”

Erik said, “Stay here with the car till I call you. Make sure your cell phone stays on.” Erik slipped stealthily off the road and through the trees down toward his cabin. Sid could hardly bear to stay behind, but he knew instructions from his boss must be strictly obeyed.

Erik came out of the woods directly behind his cabin, and slipped quietly up on the back porch. He could see in through the window, he wanted to make sure Greta was alone before he made his presence known to her. He could see into the bedroom, and there was no one there. Then he slipped quietly over to the door which had a small window, where he could see into the main room of the cabin. There she was sitting alone on the bearskin rug in front of the burning fireplace reading a book. He couldn't see anyone else in the cabin.

Greta looked nothing like he had pictured her in his mind. She was a beautiful woman, with long dark hair which rested on both of her shoulders. He wondered what the relationship between her and Otto is. As Erik stood on the porch of the cabin gazing in through the window at Greta, his mind went back to that dreadful night in England. He was just 19 years old when he met Sarah. She was also attending Oxford University. It was love at first sight for both of them.

They began to date and were together at every free moment. Sarah was from an elite upper class English family. At first they did not approve of their only daughter dating a Russian military man, but Erik warmed his way into their hearts. Just two weeks after they began dating, they became engaged and were planning on getting married after both of them finished college, which would have been in 12 months. They would have a spring wedding, and then he would take her home to Russia to meet his beloved mother and father. They were so happy at Christmas time with all the festivities and preparing for their wedding in the spring. Erik invited Sarah to go with him during Christmas break to a beautiful alpine resort in Switzerland. When Sarah told her parents what they were planning, they forbid their daughter to go off for four days vacationing with a man to whom she was not married too. Erik wanted to go so bad that he invited her mom and dad to go along as chaperones. They consented and all of them went. Sarah and Erik were on the ski slopes all day, every day they were there. Her mom and dad spent most of every day sitting around the fire at the main lodge, where Erik and Sarah joined them, exhausted at the end of each day. It was so much fun they were all sorry that it had to end, but after the four days they all boarded a plane back to England. As they were waiting for the plane to leave the gate, the pilot spoke over the intercom. He said there is a very sick man that needs immediate medical care and there is no seats left on the plane. "If we can have a volunteer to deplane and wait for twelve hours until the next flight to England is scheduled, it would be greatly appreciated and may save this man's life."

Erik looked at Sarah and she knew without a word from him that he was going to give up his seat for this stranger. She kissed him goodbye and he slowly made his way to the front of the plane to tell the captain that he would give up his seat for this man.

It was 18 hours later when Erik returned to his apartment in England. He was very tired but he must say good night to his love, which he had not seen for nearly twenty four hours. Sarah's apartment was within walking distance, so he decided to walk over and kiss her good night. When Erik arrived at Sarah's apartment he was met by her best friend Cindy, who was also her roommate. "Erik," Cindy said, "have you not heard the news? Sarah's plane went down last night in a storm and there were no survivor's. Sarah and her mother and father are all dead." Erik was so broken by the loss of his beloved Sarah that he never had any interest in any other woman to this day. That dreadful night would play over and over in his mind for the rest of his life.

Erik slowly turned the knob on the back door, and pushed it ever so gently. It was fastened from the inside. Erik knew that it was fastened only with a small piece of wood held in place with a single nail, so he drew his weapon from his holster and holding it firmly in his right hand, he threw a shoulder against the door, and it swung open with ease. Greta turned quickly to face this rugged looking red haired man with a pistol drawn and she screamed.

"I'm not here to hurt you," Erik said. "I just need to ask you some questions." Greta began to get up, half sobbing and half screaming, "I'm Erik, Otto's friend, this is my cabin."

Greta stopped screaming, but was still sobbing. "What do you want, and why do you have a gun?"

Erik put his pistol back in his holster and said, "I'm sorry, but I have to be cautious."

After nearly 30 minutes of reassuring Greta that he meant her no harm, and he was who he said he was, Greta began to calm down. Erik began to ask her some questions. "What do you know about Project Wormwood, and to what extent were you and your husband Thomas involved?" Erik said he was assisting his friend Otto in trying to find her husband and how his disappearance may somehow be linked to this mysterious project. Without revealing to Greta that he was an agent of the British intelligence service he asked her if Thomas had any ties to the military or any special government agency. Greta said to her knowledge he didn't have, she and Thomas had only been married three years and she didn't know about his life prior to their marriage. They had met while both of them were working at the International Space Station Agency. They dated a few times and Thomas asked her to marry him and she consented. They were married five months after they met. She knew nothing of Thomas' past and he never talked about it. She remembered that Thomas had to make many trips to England and other countries. He always told her never to tell Chechnikov about his trips to England, but he never told her why. Then Greta told Erik about receiving the telephone call that morning which instructed her to burn all the documents including the computer hard drive and suggested that she take the cyanide tablets, which were given to each member when they joined the project swearing their allegiance. She told him the caller warned her they are coming but did not say who they were.

Erik knew that morning someone had tipped her off, that he was coming, but whom? Greta also told him that she had some computer disks that pertained to the project. He could take them with him if he thought they would be useful. While Greta was getting the disks, Erik used his cell phone to call Sid who had been waiting with the car for two hours now. "Sid, drive down to the cabin and pick me up. Wait outside and I will be right out."

"Okay boss. Is everything all right?"

"Yes everything is fine," Erik said. Sid immediately jumped into the sedan and began the one kilometer drive down the mountain road to Erik's cabin.

When Sid arrived at the cabin Erik was still inside, so Sid left the engine running but stepped outside. He walked around the front of the sedan and leaned against the fender on the passenger side, and took out one of his thin cigars, placed it in his mouth, lit it and began to smoke it.

Erik assured Greta she wouldn't be out here alone much longer, he and Otto were securing a safe place for her to stay on the outskirts of the city of Moscow. They had found a small house that they had placed a lease on, but the current tenant wouldn't be out for three more days. Greta felt relieved.

Erik opened the front door of the cabin and walked out on the front porch. Greta could not be seen inside the semi dark cabin, but she could see clearly outside through the open door. She saw the sedan parked just in front of the cabin, and this slender somewhat disheveled little man smoking a cigar and leaning on the fender of the sedan. Greta nearly fainted. It seemed like all the blood rushed all at once to her head, and she gasped for air as she closed the door.

When Greta called Otto, her voice was trembling. Otto noticed there was something wrong, "What's the matter hon? You seem to be out of breath."

“Otto, you have got to come and get me tonight, I can't stay here any longer. My life may be endangered.” Otto could tell she was frantic, so he didn't even ask her why. He just said I'll be there before daylight, and hung up the phone.

Sid drove Erik back to the airport in Saint Petersburg to catch his flight. Sid had earlier asked Erik if he could take a couple weeks off to take his girlfriend on holiday to Paris. Erik had instructed Sid to leave the sedan at the airport parking garage in Saint Petersburg, and catch a plane from Saint Petersburg to Minsk to pick up his girlfriend, and leave from there for Paris.

As Erik was boarding the plane, he looked at Sid and said, “Enjoy yourself in Paris and you can pick up the sedan when you get back.”

Chapter 19

Otto left his office as soon as he received the call from Greta. He wanted to get to her as soon as possible. He drove faster than he usually did, and nearly missed a sharp turn on the mountain roads. He was able to break the van quick enough to negotiate the sharp turn. He arrived at the cabin just before daylight. Greta was waiting with all her things packed and ready to go. When she saw the headlights coming down the road toward the cabin, she slipped out through the backdoor and hid in the brush where she could see who was in the car. When the van pulled up in front of the cabin, and Greta saw it was Otto, she came out of her hiding place running to Otto. Otto took Greta into his arms and held her tight. She was out of breath, her heart was pounding and she was sobbing uncontrollably. “Greta, what is the matter? Did a bear try to get into the cabin or what?”

“I'll tell you all about it on our way back to the city.” Greta said, “I’ll get my suitcase and be right out.” Greta got into the van, threw her suitcase in the back, over the seat and sat very quiet, as Otto began driving back up the mountain road. “Otto,” she said after a long silence, “how well do you know your friend Erik?”

“I know him very well. He’s the head of the Department of military intelligence. His father is a three-star general in the Russian military, why do you ask?”

“He came to the cabin yesterday and broke in on me. He wanted to ask me some questions about Project Wormwood. He also asked me a lot of personal questions about Thomas, his disappearance and his involvement in the project.”

“Erik was here?” Otto said.

“Yes, but he assured me he was helping you trying to find out what happened to Thomas.”

Greta told Otto she was now afraid for her life, and she could not stay at the cabin any longer. “Why do you think Erik is a threat to you Greta?”

“Because he had someone with him that I have seen at all the project meetings. I don't know his name, but he was driving the car that Erik was in. He didn't see me, but I saw him clearly."

"Are you sure Greta that it wasn't just someone who looked like Erik's driver?"

"I am certain Otto. He has made speeches at the meetings and he always sits on the dais with Colonel Chechnikov."

Chapter 20

Erik still had a day before he was due back at his office, so he slept in till about ten o'clock. When he finally got out of bed he made coffee, and put two pieces of bread in the toaster. Then he took the computer disks he got from Greta at the cabin and slipped one of them into the drive on his computer. Erik was distracted from the viewing screen when the toast popped up. He left it running while he buttered his toast and poured himself a cup of fresh coffee.

Erik sat down at his computer and began scrolling through the lists of names. None of the names were familiar to him except Thomas and Greta Burkov. He removed the first disc and inserted the second one, and it was similar to the first one. Erik was about to eject the disk from his drive when he saw a name that was very familiar to him, Sydney Rearson.

Chapter 21

Otto awoke before Greta at about four p.m. and he went out and brought back some lunch before he awakened Greta. Otto and Greta were eating lunch as they talked about Erik. Why was he with a high-profile member of the mysterious project, at the cabin? They wondered if he knew of the involvement by his driver and confidant in the project, or would he be as surprised as they were when Otto exposes him later this evening.

Otto called Erik at home about six p.m., and asked if he would be at home this evening. Erik assured Otto he would be home and he was glad he called because he had something he wanted to show him. Otto said, "Erik, I'll be over about seven p.m. Otto told Greta she should stay in the apartment out of sight until he could get some answers about Erik.

Chapter 22

Bill Forney has been parking his car out of sight from dusk to about midnight in a small lookout area on the mountain road leading to where he saw the accident, for about a week now. He was hoping to see another military truck going to pick up some more of the radioactive cargo. Finally his persistence paid off. It was about 11:30 when a truck passed on the mountain roads where Bill was hiding. It was the same type of military truck that turned over on the mountain road. It had no markings and no escort with it as it headed in the direction the other truck was coming from. Bill waited till it was nearly out of sight, but he could still see its tail lights before he drove out of the lookout area and began to follow the truck keeping his lights off.

When the truck passed the turn where the accident occurred, it drove another six kilometers or so and turned down a road Bill was not familiar with. Bill lived about 30 kilometers east of where the truck turned off, but he was not that familiar with this area of the mountains. There were roads going in nearly every direction. Bill knew he would have to stay rather close to the truck or he would lose him on these winding roads.

Bill tried to draw a map in his mind as he followed the truck. It must've made a dozen turns already. It was getting further and further into the mountains.

When it seemed as if the truck would never reach its destination, it began to slow down. Then Bill saw a security gate just ahead that led into a fenced in compound. The truck stopped at the gate, and the passenger got out, unlocked it and swung it open to allow the truck to pass through. Then he closed and locked it, and got back into the truck and the truck began to move toward a large metal warehouse that Bill could see from the truck's lights.

Bill pulled his car off the road into a small clump of trees and got out. He took a pair of night vision binoculars and slung the strap of his camera case over a shoulder. Then he picked up his telephoto lens and with his video camera and his binoculars he started walking just off the road toward the fenced in compound. Bill moved down the fence line to get closer to the warehouse. He could see inside the compound but not inside the warehouse. The truck and four guards with automatic weapons were outside the building. He had to get inside the compound to see what was in the warehouse but he didn't see any way he could. The compound was fenced in completely with a 12 foot high fence, and it was electrified.

Bill walked cautiously down the fence line around the back of the warehouse, to see if there was any break in the fence. There wasn't a break but there was a tree with a large limb hanging over the fence. Bill thought if I can get up that tree and out on that limb he could drop down into the compound. It will be about a 12 foot drop but he thought he could do it.

After dropping over the fence into the compound Bill laid on the ground for about 15 minutes. “That was quite a drop.” Bill said. His leg was hurting a little and he had no idea how he would get back out of the compound, but he was inside now and he was going to see what was in that warehouse.

The truck had already moved inside and the guards were nowhere to be seen, probably inside too Bill thought. Bill checked his camera and binoculars to see if they were damaged when he dropped them from the limb. Everything looked okay. Bill picked up his video camera and removed it from the case, adjusted the lens and began filming his surroundings. First the entire compound, and then he focused on the warehouse, as he moved closer to the back of the building. There was a set of windows with bars on them in one side of the building. He was now just below the first window. He stood up very carefully and looked in. Bill could now see inside the well lit building, and what he saw he could hardly believe. There was a steel beam running down through the center of the building about 12 feet off the floor. Also there was a heavy five ton chain hoist located on the beam running north and south for loading heavy equipment into the truck, Bill thought. Then on one side of the building, inside a wire caged area, there were four large canisters, like nuclear waste is stored in at nuclear facilities.

Bill could see the truck and six men, the driver, his military passenger and the four armed guards. The four guards had donned radiation protection clothing and were hoisting one of the canisters into the back of the truck. The driver of the truck was sitting at a desk at the back end of the building, facing the front. He was filling out some papers. Bill could see he was the same truck driver he interviewed at the accident site.

Bill was filming everything that was going on inside the building, but what really caught his trained eye were five crates sitting alongside the truck with a computer-driven electronic device in each of them. Bill knew immediately what they were, because when the Soviet Union was dismantled, he was allowed to film the inside of a Soviet nuclear missile site. He was shown the nuclear triggering devices for each missile warhead, and they were the same type of devices he was filming now inside the building. Bill continued filming till all the canisters and crates were loaded on the truck. Then he began to think how he was going to get out of the compound without being discovered.

The truck driver started the engine and one of the guards rolled open the overhead door. The truck drove out of the building. Bill thought this is his only chance. If the guard closes the overhead door it will cut off the light from inside. Then it will be dark behind the truck and he can run from the side of the building across the space of about 20 yards, and walk out the gate behind the truck. For that to work though the guards will have to remain inside the building till the truck is through the gate and the gate is closed and locked.

The truck stopped at the gate. Bill had to run quietly and get behind the truck while the military guy was unlocking and opening the gate. He had to hope the driver didn't see him in his side view mirror. As the gate opened the truck rolled steadily through and stopped. Bill threw himself under the truck on the ground, so he could not be seen when the gate was being closed and locked. As soon as the truck moved forward, Bill threw his camera case and binoculars over next to the fence, and then he rolled over and over until he was out of the drive and next to the fence. Good, no one saw him Bill thought. "I have a blockbuster story and the video to back it up."

Chapter 23

Erik showed Otto the names on the disk and pointed out his driver Sidney among them. Sydney's name was listed in the list of the names on the second tier. Otto told Erik what Greta had told him about Sydney and that she thought Erik was a part of the project as well. Erik assured Otto that he was as surprised as they were.

The following day Erik returned to his office and planned how he would confront Sid with this information when he returned from Paris. Then Erik remembered something that Sid had said when they were near the cabin that morning. Erik remembered saying to Sid, "Drive a little closer to the cabin and find a spot to pull off the road where the car can't be spotted from the air or seen from the road."

Sid said to Erik, "I know just the place boss." How did he know just the place when neither he nor Erik had ever been there? It was Sid who tipped Greta off he must've called her from his cell phone just after I got out of the car.

Otto did not return to his office. Greta asked if he would drive out to her cabin and pick up some of her personal things that she would need when she moved to the safe house. Instead of Otto going directly to Greta's cabin, he drove to where his cabin used to be, and left his van there. He began hiking the two kilometers across the mountain to Greta's cabin. It was a pretty rough hike, but Otto was up to it. He was in good physical condition. When he reached the top of the ridge he thought he saw something move about 20 yards ahead of him. Otto crouched down and stayed very still for about five minutes. Then he picked up a good size club off the ground and held it tightly in his hand as he began to move cautiously forward. He was now about where he thought he saw something move across his path, and he stopped again and crouched down. He began looking to the left and to the right.

All of a sudden he was knocked off his feet and pushed forward. When he fell face down onto the ground he flipped over quickly onto his back to fight off his assailant with the club he still held in his hand. He struck blindly at the huge figure that was upon him and he heard a "whelp" as the club found its mark.

"Oh my God Precious, I'm so sorry." Otto said as he put his arms around his old friend, the big Irish setter began licking his face. "I thought you were killed in the blast." Otto sat there on the side of the mountain for about an hour holding back tears and holding firmly in his arms his close companion, whom he thought was lost for ever. "Come on Precious let's get down to the cabin so we can get back home. Greta will be so glad to see you."

Chapter 24

Bill Forney was in his office working with more details of the story he was going to air concerning the warehouse in the mountains, and the radioactive material he had seen being loaded onto the truck. He had decided to air this story as a government expose piece. Bill knew he would have to gather more information on the Space Station Agency and on the people involved in this covert operation, and what they were planning, before he went public. He knew there would be a lot of fallout when he aired the story, and he did not know yet how high in government it would reach.

Bill's producer, Dan, knocked and entered Bill's office. "Bill!" he said, "Here is a story that may be interesting to you."

Bill was perusing the papers on the clipboard that Dan just handed him and Dan was talking so fast that Bill looked up and said, “Dan slowdown start over, and tell me what all the excitement is about.”

Dan began slowly telling Bill about the information he was perusing on the clipboard as he showed him a newspaper he was holding in his hand. “Look Bill in section three, there is an interesting headline that reads “Two of this country's cosmonauts are dying in isolation from unknown viruses” which has medical science baffled.”

“Dan,” Bill said, “is this a virus they picked up on the International Space Station?” When Bill asked he knew that these were the two cosmonauts that had just recently returned from the space station.

“I don't know.” Dan said. “But if it is, it will make a good story for your show.”

“You do some investigating on this. Do you think you can get into their isolation ward and get interviews from the cosmonauts?”

“I know a doctor over at the hospital that will get me in to see them and get an interview. I can also pick up some background information from the doctor.”

“Go get the story then.” Bill said.

Dan was no more than 20 minutes into his interview with the doctor in his office, when a man wearing a gray suit walked in and asked Dan to step out for a few moments. He needed to speak to the doctor in private. Dan assumed that he was one of the administration's staff at the hospital and so he stepped out into the hallway as the man closed the door behind him.

Dan heard the man speaking to the doctor in a loud and agitated voice and then a heated argument began between the doctor and the staff member. After about 15 minutes of shouting and arguing the man wearing the gray suit opened the door and walked out of the office, briskly disappeared down the hall without saying a word to Dan.

The doctor looked out into the hall and motioned for Dan to come back into the office. Dan could feel the tension that was left in the office that was not there when he was interviewing the doctor. The doctor said, "Government censorship, I have never agreed with it and I hate it. Dan I can't continue our interview at this time. I was just lectured and forbidden to allow anyone into the isolation ward to meet with the cosmonauts, but you leave me your cell phone number and I will talk to you again about this matter."

Dan was at home it was after dinner and he was having a glass of vodka when his cell phone rang. "Dan," the doctor said, "are you busy?"

"No," Dan said.

"I would like to drop by and talk to you and finish our interview in private, if that's okay with you?"

"Sure what time should I expect you?"

"I'll be there about ten o'clock. I have an errand to run first."

"I'll be expecting you at or around ten." Dan said.

The doctor then went on to say, "In case something happens and I'm unable to make it, be sure and check your mail box tomorrow morning. I have sent you a package of information. I think you'll find very interesting."

Ten o'clock came and went. Dan continued to wait for his friend the doctor until about 12 o'clock, and then he decided he wasn't coming so he went to bed.

The following morning Dan made himself a cup of coffee, sat down and turned on the television to watch the morning news. The anchor of the morning news program said to his television audience, "This just in, a prominent doctor was found dead at the train station last night. Now we're going to take you to the reporter at the scene to get a live report." The news reporter was standing with his mike in hand waiting for a prompt from his station, and then he began his report. A prominent medical doctor was found dead at about 1:30 this morning. Here in the train station by the payphone area. It has all the appearance of a homicide according to the medical examiner. He died at about ten o'clock last night. His name is not being revealed by the police until his family can be notified. Our television crew was here on the scene just after the body was discovered this morning, and we did manage to get a still photograph of the body while the medical examiner was examining him." The photo was flashed on the TV screen.

Dan nearly dropped his cup of coffee when he saw the photograph of his friend, the doctor on the screen. He listened for more information, but that was all the information that the reporter had, and he turned it back to the anchor on the morning news. Immediately Dan called Bill Forney, "Bill something big is developing around that cosmonauts' story. I won't be in the office until this after noon. Then I will tell you what I've learned, but I believe it's going to be a very big story."

Dan could hardly wait until the mail ran. He was anxious to see what the doctor had sent him, and to see what would cause someone to be so threatened that they would have to kill him for it.

The mail arrived at about 12:30. Dan met the mailman at the door, and received a large manila envelope with no return address on it. He then sat down and opened the sealed envelope. There were several sheets of paper with notes written by hand on them. "Dan," the doctor wrote, "I am fearful for my life since they interrupted our interview yesterday."

“I have raised some serious questions at the hospital concerning the condition of the two cosmonauts in the isolation ward. I was told by the doctor treating them that he was not to tell anyone who inquired about the cosmonauts. That they had been infected with an unknown virus on the space station and were being kept in isolation until it could be determined whether the virus was infectious, and whether there was an antibiotic to control it. I went to the ward to examine the cosmonauts myself. Since I am a senior staff member I was able to get in. There I discovered it is not a virus that they suffer from, but something much more sinister. I have seen it many times before since the accident at Chernobyl, the cosmonauts are without doubt dying of a very high dosage of radiation exposure.”

“From the condition of their bodies, they would have had to been exposed to a higher level than the men closest to the core at Chernobyl at the time of the accident. And the only place they could have been exposed was either during the trip to the space station or after their arrival. The mystery, there is no high-level radiation that they could be exposed to. Either in the space agency building or during their trip to the station or at the space station itself.”

“One of the cosmonauts told me, because he knows he is dying, that they were exposed to the contents of a canister that they were delivering to the space station when it was accidentally punctured as they were offloading it onto the station. He did not know what was in the canister but it had radioactive materials sign painted on it. It had top-secret classified material stenciled on the canister."

"My partner and I were supposed to stay at the station for a three month tour, but after we arrived we became so sick after one week. Instead of sending the other cosmonauts home who were ending their tour, we had to be taken off instead and placed here in the isolation ward. We were both instructed by the agency official not to talk to anyone about the canister, because it was highly classified."

"Dan, both of these men know that they will be dead in less than a wee. There's nothing in medical science that can save them, and I guess that's why they were willing to talk to me. They told me that they and the other cosmonauts have delivered at least a hundred classified packages to the space station in the last 12 months. Many of them were like the same large canisters that we were delivering. All the cosmonauts in the program were told by the agency that all the packages had to be delivered via a Russian cargo run. They must be delivered prior to the Americans being able to redeploy their space shuttles to the space station carrying their own astronauts. They also confided in me that on the last mission to the station two of Russia's top scientists and two of our nuclear physicist engineers were sent to the station, and they remained there and are there even now."

"They told me the short time they were there the engineers and scientists were assembling several unusual devices all of which was classified. None of the cosmonauts were allowed to be a part of."

"I do not know what covert operation is going on at the International Space Station Agency, but you are in a position to investigate it. If there is anything that should be revealed to the public, you are the one that can expose it."

"And if you begin an investigation, be very careful to protect yourself at all times. Trust no one in either the military intelligence or the government.

Chapter 25

Erik was in his office when he heard voices being raised and a lot of loud commotion coming from his father's office, just across the hall from his. He got up and walked across the hall and into the reception area. He noticed that his father's secretary was not in the office. As he moved close to the inner door he could hear what was being said.

Erik heard his father saying to someone in his office in an agitated voice, "The agency is out of control. When we agreed to be a part of Project Wormwood we insisted, and you agreed, that we would not use the military nor would there be any violence. We only agreed to speak at staged demonstrations, and take part in negotiations. If you can't get the agency under control, I will end the project now. Your attack helicopters could have killed my son when they blew up the cabin wrong cabin. I was never aware that the military was being used to intimidate or frighten people.

The other man spoke and said, “It was an honest mistake there was a mix-up in the coordinates of the target. Your son was supposed to be at the cabin and have removed Mrs. Burkov for questioning. Both he and Mrs. Burkov were supposed to be on their way back to the city before we struck the target. I assure you, neither your son nor Mrs. Burkov was ever intended to be the target.

Erik couldn't believe what he was hearing. He slipped quietly across the hall to his own office, but he stood at the window of his office to see if he could see the man whom his father was speaking to, as he left. After about 15 minutes the man left his father's office. He was a large man with a full gray mustache wearing a military uniform with the markings of a full bird colonel. Erik thought, “Sid will be back from his vacation next week and he will have a lot of questions to answer.”

Chapter 26

Gentlemen General Boris Roskov said, as he stood at the podium in front of the Security Council of the United Nations, “It is a great honor and a grand privilege that my request was honored to address this august body. I'm deeply humbled to be here. Let me say, my mission here today is not to criticize anyone of you gentlemen and or the leadership of the nation's you represent, but rather I'm here today to challenge all of you to come together and work as one world government. It is the only way to overcome the seemingly insurmountable obstacles that are before us in this century, and must be conquered if we are to survive on our planet and live in peace with man and nature.”

“Since the former Soviet Union was dismantled, and the Baltic States, and many other of the Soviet block states have chosen to separate themselves from mother Russia many changes have taken place in Russia, East Germany, and all the former Soviet block states. Many of these changes as you know have been brought about by the introduction of democracy and the fall of communism."

"As you gentlemen are aware there is a large quantity of enriched weapons grade plutonium that is missing and unaccounted for from several nuclear facilities in the former Soviet Union. There is also several nuclear missile sites with anti-ballistic missiles armed with nuclear warheads that are under the control and authority of unstable governments. Many of them are new and have very tenuous leadership after their break from the Soviet Union. At any time these weapons of mass destruction could fall into the hands of terrorist extremists, if they have not already."

"Russia and the United States have stockpiles of nuclear warheads installed on anti-ballistic missiles which are capable of reaching any place on earth. Together these two nations have more than enough weapons of mass destruction to destroy the entire earth and every living creature on it. It is for that reason that we must work together to stop this madness and begin a serious disarmament in all nations."

General Boris Roskov continued his speech for over two hours. As he rambled on about how there must be a parity of the nations of the world, especially when it affects the energy supply of the whole earth. "There must be world authority and world dialogue concerning the depletion of the ozone layer and other serious matters such as global warming, food distribution, and economical development. We must no longer allow a few western nations to with disregard of all other nations of the world. To use up as much as 85% of the earth's energy supply, while all other developing nations are lacking enough natural resources to survive. Only because these fledgling nations are not wealthy enough to purchase the needed oil and gas, building materials, food supplies and other of the earth's commodities that they need to grow and develop economically. The few nations who hold the power, and have access to the largest share of the earth's natural resources, also have an insationable appetite for 85 % of the earth's energy as well. The indiscriminate use of these resources has led to the pollution of earth's air and water supply, and is creating an abnormal change in the weather patterns, as well as the continual depletion of the ozone layer that surrounds the earth and protects its entire people from deadly rays from the sun."

"Since this agency was formed to promote and assure peace among the nations of the world, there has been constant and chaotic hostility between nations. The flashpoint for much of this hostility is directly related to the worst travesty of international justice that was ever to be initiated and approved by this agency. When the ruling nations of the world, by consent, allowed the millions of Arab populations, to be forcefully removed from their homes and their lands in Palestine and forced to live in a hostile desert and wilderness area while their homes, their farms, and their lands were given to another ethnic race, with not so much as compensation. That gentleman was the highest degree of genocide at the largest scale that was ever perpetrated on this earth."

"To restore a continual peace on this earth the United Nations must come together and see the populations of the earth through a worldview. You must take steps now to right many wrongs and to give to all races and ethic groups full parity with the rich and powerful nations of the world."

"Thank you gentlemen for allowing me to speak to you and for your attentiveness to my words, I beg of you to act now or it may be too late."

The same day General Boris Roskov was addressing the United Nations Security Council, lower tier members of Project Wormwood were arranging and organizing demonstrations in nearly every capital city in the European Union, the United States and Russia. These demonstrations were on the same order as the general was proclaiming in his speech at the United Nations.

Chapter 27

It was late in the evening, Otto and Greta had just finished eating dinner. As Greta was removing the dishes from the table, and Precious was busy devouring all the table scraps the phone rang. “Hello?” Otto said.

“Otto this is Erik, can you stop by my office in the morning about 8:00?”

“Sure.” Otto said, “Do you want to tell what it is about?”

“I’ll tell you in the morning when you get here.” Erik said.

Otto arrived at Erik's office early and was sitting in the reception area drinking a cup of hot coffee, and passing the time with Erik’s secretary, when Erik arrived. “Good morning hon.” Erik said to his secretary as he walked briskly toward his office door, and motioned for Otto to follow him. "Sit down Otto, and thank you for coming." Erik said, as he pushed the button on his intercom. "Hold all my calls and back up all my appointments for about two hours." Erik told his secretary.

"What is it?" said Otto.

"Our friend Bill from the TV station stopped by to see me yesterday. Four hours we went over some very interesting and disturbing information that his producer, Dan, stumbled onto by accident." Erik told Otto about the doctor who was killed, the two cosmonauts, the isolation ward at the hospital, and the contents of the envelope the doctor sent Dan before he was killed. "Otto, all this is somehow connected to the agency and this Project Wormwood. Somehow I feel that our national security is in jeopardy." Erik then told Otto about the conversation he overheard at his father's office.

"As the head of the department of military intelligence, and a close friend, I am asking you to take on what may be a very dangerous assignment. I want you to check every document, every procurement invoice, and every cargo manifest that is remotely connected with the International Space Station Agency. See if you can find out anything about our mysterious colonel. I think he is the one that was in my father's office."

Otto sat in his chair looking completely stunned at what he had just learned from Erik. “Sure I can do what you ask.” Otto said. “Has Sid returned from his vacation yet?”

“No.” Erik said, “Sometime next week, and when he does, he has a lot of questions to answer.”

Chapter 28

The plane touched down on the runway at Saint Petersburg airport and taxied to the gate. Sid had a great two weeks in Paris with his girlfriend, but now it is back to work and the same old grind.

Sid made his way through the international terminal toward the baggage area. He thought, "I believe it is time to get married and settle down. I have some money saved and with the salary Erik pays me, and the little compensation I get from Colonel Chechnikov. I can make it quite well. I think when I get home tonight I'll make a phone call to Minsk, and propose to my girlfriend. I think she will say yes. After all she was hinting about it all the time we were in Paris. We had a great time while we were there."

With the thought of marriage on his mind Sid retrieved his baggage and headed for the parking lot where he had parked Erik's sedan two weeks ago. As Sid drove off he had an uneasy feeling. He did know what it was, and it just kind of nagged at him. He started thinking about that night in October when Colonel Chechnikov called him at home and told him Erik was a British agent, and that he was investigating the wormwood project. "He was going in the morning to arrest Greta Burkov at her cabin and bring her in for questioning. She will undoubtedly tell him all that he needs to know about Project Wormwood. He will probably have you drive him there. Take him to her cabin in the mountains. You stay back out of the way. I will send a military helicopter with a number of soldiers and arrest him and bring him in. We will hold him under house arrest until the project can be executed."

When I gave the colonel the coordinates to the cabin, I never dreamed that he wanted to kill Erik. Although I felt uneasy, the same feeling I am feeling now. Like something is wrong. I gave the colonel the wrong coordinates, so it would take time for his pilot to find the cabin, if he found it at all. I even told Erik we should leave an hour earlier than we had planned, so we would have time to get to the cabin, pick up Mrs. Burkov, and leave before the chopper pilot ever found the cabin. I never dreamed they were going to fire missiles into the cabin or that there was another cabin two kilometers north, just over the ridge from the Burkov's.

Erik is a good friend, British agent are not. The colonel may have fabricated that story. When I get back to Moscow I'm going to Erik's office first thing in the morning, and tell him all I know about Chechnikov and the project. When I signed on to work for the project there was never to be any violence. The colonel has become a rogue leader and the project has been taken over and changed to promote his personal agenda.

As Sid continued driving toward the city of Moscow, and home he could not shake that uneasy feeling that was gnawing at his gut. He began to let his mind wander back to the first time he had met Colonel Chechnikov.

He was sitting in the reception area of his then boss General Boris Roskov, waiting to drive him to the airport. When this tall Soviet military officer with a thick gray mustache walked in and sat down next to him. Since his days serving in the KGB, Sid was always leery about all Soviet military officers, because he had investigated and informed on so many of them. He never knew when one of them or their relatives would meet up with him and take revenge. So he never spoke to the officer until the officer spoke to him and then he was very cautious of what he said in response. At first it was just small talk about the weather, if he had any family, how long had he been the general's driver, because Sid was wearing the uniform that a military driver would wear when working. Then the conversation began to tilt toward politics. At first the officer was discussing politics of the Russian government, and then he turned his discussion to a world view.

Sid was becoming more comfortable talking with this gentleman, although he was still a little uneasy and kept his guard up. He kept looking at the watch on his wrist hoping that the general would step out of his office and they would be on their way to the airport. Finally after sitting and talking with the officer for about an hour, the general stepped out of his office and greeted the officer, "Good afternoon Colonel Chechnikov, how long have you been here? I didn't know you were here. My secretary had to take the day off because of a family emergency. I am on my way to the airport and will be out of my office for the next two weeks. Why don't you ride along with me to the airport and we can talk. My driver will bring you back into the city after my plane leaves."

On the way to the airport the general and the officer talked about a number of things, but their main conversation was concerning this special project. They both seemed to be involved in it, calling wormwood. The officer was giving General Roskov some dates and information about world conferences, rallies, and demonstrations he would like for him to attend and speak. The general seemed to become a little agitated when the officer insisted he attend all of these demonstrations.

I remember when we arrived at the airport and let General Roskov out of the car. Before I could take off again the colonel got out of the back seat of the car and got in the front on the passenger side. It made me a little nervous because I was always used to my passenger riding in the back as the general always did.

All the way back into the city the colonel seemed to be interrogating Sid. He asked how long he had worked for the general, how long he had known him and other personal questions. Sid had become more comfortable and less intimidated by the colonel the more they talked. Until he began to tell him more personal things about himself and the colonel showed more than a passing interest when Sid revealed that he had worked with intelligence with the KGB agency. He began to ask more questions about the Soviet intelligence community. Sid told him that the general had taken over the remnants of the KGB and their intelligence. When the Soviet government collapsed and communism was replaced with a less totalitarian form of government. He also told him that the general was looking for a good man to place in charge of the new intelligence agency. He had mentioned his son, which was attending college in England, as a candidate.

They arrived at the address in the city that the colonel had given Sid. Before getting out of the car the colonel wrote his telephone number on a piece of paper and gave it to Sid.

Sid was rather surprised a few weeks later when he got a call from Colonel Chechnikov at his apartment in Moscow.

"Sid," the colonel said, "This is Colonel Chechnikov, are you going to be free tomorrow? I would like you to come over to my office at the Kremlin and listen to a proposal I have to make to you."

"Yes I think I can do that." Sid said. "What time do you want me there?"

"How about 10:00 A.M., is that too early?"

"No that would be fine. I will see you in the morning."

When Sid arrived at the colonel's office he was a little surprised. He expected a large well lit office in a prime location inside the headquarters of the Kremlin. After all he was a Soviet Military officer. According to all the battle ribbons he displayed on his uniform, he was highly decorated. Sid thought it would make him well respected and favored in the Kremlin.

Instead the colonel's office was a very small corner room with no windows. Boxes that were packed for moving were stacked on the floor and on top of a well worn table in the corner. The lighting was so dim Sid could hardly make out the features of the large man sitting at the desk in the center of the room. “Come in and sit down.” the colonel said, “You will have to excuse the condition of my office. They are in the process of moving me over to my new headquarters at the International Space Station Agency. I have been assigned to head that agency. It’s quite a promotion for me.”

“Thank you for coming on such short notice.” the colonel said, “Would you like a cup of coffee?”

“No,” Sid said, “I am fine.”

“Let’s get right to the reason for you being here. I would like for you to come and work for me. Let me introduce you to some of my colleagues. They have nothing to do with the military, but we have formed a very important organization, which I think you would fit into very well. With your KGB background you would be an essential asset to the organization.”

Sid was curious about what this colonel was offering him. He said to the colonel, “I would like to hear more about this before I consider making any kind of a decision.”

“I understand, but I cannot reveal too much about our organization to you until I know more about you.”

“I would have to talk to General Roscov to see if he would release me from my position that I have with him before making any decision.”

The colonel interrupted Sid, "It would not be necessary for you to leave your position as the general's driver. In fact I would rather that you did not. I have it on the best authority that the general is about to transfer you over to his son Erik, whom he is grooming to step in and take over the whole Russian intelligence community. It is for this very reason that I would like for you to work for our organization undercover and continue your position as driver and confidant of the general and his son Erik. I know this must sound mysterious to you Sid and may even remind you of the old Soviet Union KGB days when you were involved in gathering intelligence undercover. Well Sid, it's nothing like that. In fact just to set your mind at ease, I must tell you that General Roskov is one of the primary spokesmen for our organization."

"If you are free this weekend I would like for you to accompany me to one of our organizations rallies in the city of Minsk. Then you will have a better understanding of our organization, its purpose, and its goals."

Before Sid answered the colonel he thought about the sweet young girl that he had been corresponding with, who lived in the city of Minsk. If he went with the colonel he would be able to meet this sweet young thing and perhaps move their relationship to a higher level.

"Yes, I will be free." Sid said, "I would love to attend your rally to get a better understanding of what your organization and the people in it are all about. This would help me to make my decision."

Before he left the colonel's office, the colonel had made arrangements for Sid to accompany him that weekend on his flight to Minsk.

Sid was excited that the colonel was interested in him and he was looking forward to the coming weekend. Not only would it be an interesting trip, he would no doubt meet with some very interesting people, but he was also looking forward to meeting face-to-face with the young girl he had been communicating with.

It was about 7 A.M. when the colonel's car arrived and picked Sid up at his apartment. The driver took directly to the airport. When they arrived the colonel had already boarded the plane and save this seat next to him for Sid. The flight was only about an hour, and the colonel said very little during that time. He kept himself busy going over a lot of papers that he carried in his briefcase. When they landed in Minsk there was a car waiting to take them downtown to the city square, where the rally was going to be held.

When they arrived at the city square, people had already started to gather. They were looking at all the large signs that had been erected around the city square which depicted all the environmental issues. Sid was trying to take it all in. He did not know what to make of it all, but he was anxious to learn what this mysterious organization was all about.

There were no seats in the city square, and as the crowd began to enlarge it became standing room only, as they pressed up toward the makeshift platform that had been erected there. It was about 10 A.M. when a man dressed in a suit approached the podium and took the microphone. Tapping it, "Is this on?" Then he addressed the crowd that gathered. First by telling them how much he appreciated their being there, and then how important it was for them to be there. He introduced himself as a university professor and an eco-scientist. Whose primary interest was to help preserve our planet for future generations. After he had spoken for about 15 minutes on many ecological concerns, he then introduced Colonel Chechnikov as the primary spokesman for the organization.

Sid listened intensely as the colonel spoke to the crowd for about two hours. There were bursts of applause from time to time from the audience. What the colonel said made a lot of sense. It seemed that there had come together a large number of highly recognized eco-scientists from all over the world. Joined themselves together to form this organization, whose sole purpose was to do whatever was necessary to reverse the destruction of our planet by pollution of air and water and land by the large industrial nations of the world. The colonel said,

"The heads of government of these environment destroying nations could not be trusted to reverse, or even arrest their destructive practices and policies. We must then use whatever means we have at our disposal whether it be by force or by political persuasion. We must stop the destruction of the ecology of our planet."

After the rally ended the colonel took Sid and introduced him to many of the scientists of the organization. After that the colonel said he would be tied up for about the next two hours in organizational meetings. If Sid would like, he could use his car and driver to take him around the city to see the sights. Sid accepted the colonel's offer. This would be the perfect time for him to meet with his girlfriend. He phoned her and said he had about two hours and asked where they could meet for lunch. She chose a small delicatessen in the center of the city and gave him the directions. She would meet him there in 30 minutes.

Sid was thinking about what he would say to Erik in the morning, when a large military truck came up behind him and bumped the back of the sedan. The truck hit so hard, Sid almost lost control of the car. The winding mountain road was too narrow for the truck to get around him, but he knew that the mountain road turned into a four-lane highway, going into Moscow, about five kilometers ahead. The truck hit the bumper again and again, but Sid was able to stay just ahead of him. He kept the sedan under control. Sid thought, “Who is this, and why are they trying to run me off the road? There's a sharp curve coming just at the bottom of the hill on the mountain road, just before it meets the four-lane highway. I'll have to slow the car down to negotiate that curve. It will give the truck driver the opportunity to catch me again.

Chapter 29

Erik was sound asleep when the phone rang, and woke him up. “Erik Roskov?” The caller asked.

“Yes this is, who's calling?”

“This is Sergeant Rymer, of the National Highway Police. Sir, do you own a sedan with a license inscription government 01?”

“Yes I do, why? Has it been stolen?”

“I'm not sure the sergeant said, but it has been in a bad accident. It seems it ran off a mountain road just before it reached the highway coming from Saint Petersburg.

“How about the driver,” Erik said, “was he injured?

“I'm afraid the driver's dead.” the sergeant said. “The car is badly burned and we're trying to identify the driver now. We think we may be able to identify him from some luggage that we found inside the trunk. That is about the only thing that wasn't burned."

"We will call you at this number as soon as we get the remains of the car back up on the road and retrieve the driver's body."

"Here, I'll give you my cell phone number." Erik said. "Call me on it. I am leaving Moscow now and I will be there in two hours. I am the director of military intelligence, wait till I get there, I'll identify the body of the driver."

Erik arrived at the scene about 4 A.M. The police were waiting for him. They had winched the car up on the roadway. The body of the driver was lying on the side of the road covered with a tarp.

A small framed man wearing a police uniform with sergeant stripes approached him, "I am Sergeant Rymer, and you must be Erik Roskov." Erik nodded and walked over to the tarp covered body with the sergeant. Another police officer pulled back the tarp to reveal a severely burned body. There were still enough of the features on the body that was intact that Erik knew at once it was his friend Sid.

"What happened?" asked Erik.

"It looks like the driver may have fallen asleep and missed the curve. The car caught fire after it turned over several times. There are tire skid marks on the road. So he probably woke up just as he reached the curve and tried to brake the car, but he was going too fast."

Erik walked around behind the car when he noticed something peculiar. He called the sergeant over and asked him if the car had drove headlong down the mountain, and had it flipped over and over again or had it rolled over on its side? The Sergeant said the car appeared to have gone headfirst down the mountain, and as it dragged across the rocks it ruptured the fuel tank. The last hundred feet or so, it rolled over and over till it reached the bottom then it burst into flames. There it must have been nearly a full tank of fuel for it to burn as much as it did.

"Thanks." Erik said and the sergeant walked away. Erik was still wondering how the rear bumper got so severely bent, and where did the green paint come from that was on the bumper? It looked like something green had scraped the bumper of the car.

Erik and his father claimed Sid's body and arranged for the funeral. Sid's girlfriend came down from Minsk and with Sid's mother, and except for Erik, and Gen. Ivan Roskov, and a few friends of Sid from the old KGB no one else attended the funeral.

Chapter 30

Erik returned to his office after the funeral in the afternoon, to catch up on some paperwork. He was about to leave when Otto called, “Erik? I found something that may be of interest to your investigation. Can you come over to the safe house this evening? Greta will prepare us a nice dinner and then we can talk.”

“Sure,” Erik said, “what time?”

“We will have dinner about seven.”

“Okay, I'll be there a little before seven.” Erik said.

After eating a well-prepared dinner, Otto and Erik retired to the living room while Greta cleared the table in the dining room and Precious ate all the left overs. “What have you found Otto?” Erik said.

"Well I'm not sure if it is important to your investigation or not, but I thought it was interesting enough to tell you. I was looking through some procurement files from the agency like you asked me to do. I came across a rather interesting procurement document. Look at this, they are purchasing enough dry food and bottled water to supply at least ten or fifteen people for a year or more. The reason it seems strange to me is I have been reviewing their procurement documents for food and water for the space station for over two years now. Erik, they have never purchased more than two or three months supply of food and water for two cosmonauts that our on tour. They are now stockpiling large quantities of supplies on the station and I'm wondering why."

Erik told Otto and Greta that he suspected Sid was murdered. That it had something to do with his involvement in Project Wormwood. Erik then revealed to Otto and Greta that he was working undercover for the British intelligence agency, and his assignment was to find out what Project Wormwood was. If it was of national security interest, and if so who was behind it and how was the International Space Station involved. Then he told Greta that her husband. "Thomas was also working with the MI5 agency, and he is the person who made the first report to the agency concerning the project. Shortly after that he dropped out of sight. We have reason to suspect that his cover was discovered and reported to the colonel, who probably had him killed. I'm very sorry Greta." Erik said. "It is hard for me to accept, but somehow my own father is involved in this covert project. He does not know I work for the British intelligence, but I'm going to find out what his involvement in the project is. If it is as sinister and covert as Colonel Chechnikov seems to be, I will have to arrest him along with all the others when we finally expose this mysterious project.

Otto and Greta could hardly believe what Erik had just told them about Thomas and himself. They both knew it must be true for Erik to expose himself as he did to them.

Chapter 31

Dan drove back to the hospital to see if he could get an interview with the two cosmonauts in the isolation ward by saying it would be a good human interest story. When he arrived at the hospital there were military guards armed with automatic weapons at every door blocking his entrance. He returned to the TV studio to tell Bill what he had seen. Bill was still working on the truck story when Dan came into his office. After Dan told Bill what happened Bill said, "We need some more background on this story before I can run it. I would like for you to go back to the warehouse where I shot the film, and see if you can get more footage for the show. If you can get inside the warehouse that would be great, but Dan, don't put yourself in any unnecessary danger. After Bill drew

Dan a map and gave him additional instructions, Dan left the studio.

Chapter 32

Otto and Greta had very recently become a couple in a serious relationship. They were living together at the safe house. They were both relieved and saddened when Erik broke the news to them that Thomas, Greta's husband, was most likely dead. Otto was still reviewing all the documents that came through his office concerning the International Space Station Agency, and reporting his findings to Erik. He was looking for any unusual procurement. It was December now and the agency was preparing to send two more cosmonauts to the space station. The two cosmonauts they were sending had never been on the space station, but they were the only ones that were ready which could relieve the two cosmonauts that were there now. These two had been there now five months. They were scheduled to be relieved by the two cosmonauts whom had to be taken off the space station after the accident with the radioactive canister. The two new cosmonauts were briefed about their duties and were told that all they learned in their briefing and about the cargo they were delivering to the space station was classified and top-secret. They were told they had three days to prepare for launch, and during this time they were instructed by Colonel Chechnikov not to leave the agency's grounds and to talk to no one in the news media. During the three days of waiting the cosmonauts watched the loading of the cargo. They saw tons of food and water being loaded onto the cargo carrier for the trip to the space station. They also saw several large canisters stamped with the radioactive material sign, they were being loaded as cargo along with several crates of computerized equipment, a dozen or so automatic rifles, and several boxes of rounds of ammunition.

The day before they were scheduled for launch the two cosmonauts grew anxious of their mission and a little bit frightened by what they had seen as cargo. They decided to slip into an office at the agency unawares, and gain access to a computer terminal. They searched for an e-mail address for the military intelligence, when they found an address they sent a message, "Something strange going on at Space Station Agency. We are scheduled to depart for space station at 6 A.M. Cargo we are delivering is classified radioactive material, automatic weapons, tons of food and water, and crates of computerized equipment, please investigates. Do not reveal this information to Colonel Chechnikov, as it would place our lives in danger."

The next day after the cosmonauts were launched, and on their way to the International Space Station with the cargo, Erik was in his office checking his e-mail files when he saw the message sent by the cosmonauts. He immediately called his friend Otto, and asked if it would be okay for him to stop by at the safe house to review all the information they had learned about Project Wormwood and Colonel Chechnikov. Otto said we will be expecting you for dinner about 7 P.M.

Otto and Greta were discussing all they had learned about the Project Wormwood and Colonel Chechnikov, while they were preparing dinner for their guest. Erik arrived at about 6:30. While Greta continued preparing dinner, Otto and Erik began exchanging information on what each of them had learned. Erik was just about to tell Otto about the e-mail message he received from the cosmonauts when Greta called them to the table for dinner. By this time Greta had come to trust Erik, and they were able to speak openly about the project. After dinner Greta went with Otto and Erik to the living room to talk. She decided she could clear the table and wash the dishes after Erik left. Erik told them about the e-mail message, and said it is too late to stop the launch. I am opening a full investigation, so we will keep what we know under wraps until my father returns from his trip abroad, which will be in about a week. I am going to confront my father and see how he is involved in the project and what he knows.

Chapter 33

It had been two days since the cosmonauts were launched to the space station when an aide of Colonel Chechnikov came hurriedly into the Colonel's office at the agency, and gave him this news. "One of the two cosmonauts had been found tied and gagged, and locked inside a maintenance closet in one of the offices at the agency."

The colonel was furious. "How could this happen, and who did we send to the space station? The station is not scheduled to contact the control center until Saturday."

Chapter 34

Erik was in his office early Wednesday morning. His father was scheduled to be back in his office next Monday, and Erik wanted to put together all the files and the discs he got from Greta, and the disk he got from Otto. He wanted to make sure he had all the information he needed. Including the information Bill had given him, and his suspicion that Sid had been murdered, when he questioned his father.

While Erik was assembling all this information he noticed the icon on his computer flashing indicating he had mail. He clicked the mouse to open his e-mail and discovered a new message that was very troubling. The message read, "Erik, I am on my way to the space station. I took the place of one of the cosmonauts. I must try and stop this madman's plan to take control of, and use the International Space Station to promote his personal agenda and perhaps become a danger to the entire world. I have reason to believe they are assembling one or more nuclear devices on the space station please contact Mr. O'Donnell. Signed Thomas Burkov."

If the message had not mentioned Mr. O'Donnell, Erik would not have believed the message was from Thomas Burkov. He knew no one else had knowledge of O'Donnell, but he and Thomas Burkov.

Chapter 35

Dan had gone to the warehouse as instructed by Bill, but when he arrived he discovered an empty metal building with no security fence and no guards. He took some footage and returned to the studio to tell Bill what he had found.

Bill told Dan, "We will open the show in the morning and run a teaser trailer concerning the exposé we are running tomorrow morning. We will run just enough footage to tease our audience, and run the photo of the mysterious colonel, but obscure his face. We will tell our audience to be sure and watch the show tomorrow to learn the colonel's identification, and the exposé of the century. Bill left the studio about 8 P.M. the following day after reporting to his morning show audience that tomorrow's show would be a feature exposé, and ran the teasing trailer, Dan had put together. Upon leaving the studio Bill found lying on the roof of his car in the parking garage, a package addressed to him. Bill picked up the package and got into his car. He opened the package very carefully not knowing what he might find. There was a file folder in the package, and inside the folder were some photographs. Bill began looking through the photographs and he was astonished. The first photograph in the folder was the backyard of Bill's home in the mountains. He had a large backyard where he kept two large Doberman pincers for security. His entire backyard was fenced in, and the fence line ran about 250 feet long extending from the back of his house to the edge of a sheer cliff that dropped about 1000 feet below.

Bill knew in order to take this photograph the photographer had to be inside the fence in the backyard with the camera pointing toward the back of his house, but how could that be? The next picture Bill saw was his 16 year old daughter, Jenny, getting out of the Jacuzzi on their back porch. She was wearing nothing but a small bikini bathing suit. Bill's anger began to rise when he saw a photograph of Jenny while she was undressing. It was taken through her bedroom window. By this time Bill was shaking so hard with anger he could barely hold the photographs. There were other photographs of his daughter completely naked, others of her and her mother leaving the driveway in their car, and others of his daughter at the school she attended.

Then Bill found a message written on a piece of paper underneath the photographs. The message said, “If you run the exposé story, or reveal the colonel’s identity, you will be putting your family in grave jeopardy. Cancel the story and destroy all the documents and camera footage, as well as still photos you have. Forget any of this ever existed.”

Bill was so shaken he could hardly drive his car home. “How did they get past the dogs?” Bill thought. Then he remembered about a week ago, his wife had called him at the studio and told him that something was wrong with the dogs. They were acting lethargic. She wanted to know if she should call the veterinarian, and take them in for a checkup. Bill instructed his wife to call the veterinarian, and see what his instructions were. The veterinarian told her that there's no need bring them in today. It may be just something that they ate. Perhaps a toad they found in the yard. Wait until tomorrow morning and if there's no change in them, then bring them in, and we'll give them a full checkup.

“It was something they ate.” Bill thought, “Someone must have baited them with some kind of tranquilizer in some meat, because they were okay the next morning.”

On the drive home Bill was raging inside, and he became very frightened for his wife and their daughter. “Those rotten thugs, to stoop low enough to take pictures of my 16 year old daughter undressing and completely naked. To what extremes will they go to keep this story from being exposed? Do I dare tell my wife? No, it would worry her to death. I will cancel the story and take my wife and daughter on holiday out of Russia. Until I can think this through, and no story is worth the safety of my family." He then called Dan on his cell phone. "Dan I decided not to run the story, I just don't have enough factual evidence to make it a real exposé. Put together another piece for tomorrows show. I'll explain it somehow to our audience."

"Okay Bill," Dan said, "you're the boss."

Chapter 36

It was Saturday morning. Colonel Chechnikov was at the mission control center with a few hand-picked operators when the message came in from the space station. “Mission control emergency, go to encrypted code scramble mode, this message is for Colonel Chechnikov only.”

The colonel looked at the operator and waved his hand, and said, “Leave it. I'll decide who should hear the message.”

The caller said, “We have a situation at the station that you should know about. When the cargo transporter docked at the station and the cosmonauts were unloading the cargo. One of the cosmonauts accidentally opened a hatch to the outside and was swept out into space without a tether line. Colonel, he is gone, and we have no way of retrieving him.”

“This is Colonel Chechnikov, code clearance CXLB.”

“Code number verified.” said the space station caller, “Go-ahead colonel, we are in scramble mode here.”

“Give me the identification number of the cosmonaut that remains on the station.”

“Just a moment colonel, I’ll get it for you. 0811269.” said the caller.

The colonel looked at the identification number of the cosmonaut that was found tied and gagged at the agency. “0811269, good.” said the colonel, “The problem has solved itself. There's nothing we can do about it now. I will notify the man's family and take care of all the arrangements here. I will want a full report in 24 hours, Colonel Chechnikov signing off.”

Chapter 37

Erik sent a message on a back channel to Mr. O'Donnell to tell him about the contact that he had from Thomas. He received a message confirming that O'Donnell knew of Thomas's attempt to get on the inside of the space station. Thomas had made contact with the department five days ago O'Donnell said.

Erik arrived unannounced at the safe house the following day. He told Otto and Greta about the contact that Thomas had made with him, and that he was trying to find a way to get onto the space station. Otto and Greta turned ashen white when they heard that Thomas was alive. They were speechless. They told Erik they did not know what they were going to do now, but they thanked him for telling them.

Erik was driving back to his place and thinking about all that had taken place over the last two and a half months, and how he was going to interrogate his beloved father Monday morning. “What if he has to place him under arrest?” he thought. “What his beloved mother would have thought of him?”

Greta and Otto talked through the night. They both were very much in love with each other. They both agreed, no matter what happens now, even if Thomas reappears, they are determined to stay together.

Monday morning Erik arrived at his office early, he wanted to make sure he had everything he needed before he talked to his father, who'd be back in his office around 10 A.M. He watched from the reception area, chatting with his secretary who came in at eight, until he saw his father enter his office across the hall at about 9:30. Erik gave his father time to settle in, get a cup of coffee, and go through his mail before he went to see him.

“Good morning son, sit down and let me tell you about my trip.” General Roskov said to his son.

Erik interrupted his father, “Father we have some very important things to discuss. Why don’t you tell your secretary to hold all your calls, so we're not interrupted.”

“We won't be interrupted son. My secretary won't be in the office today. Now what is so important you couldn't tell me on the phone last night when we talked?”

“I don't know where to begin, so let's begin with you telling me how you are involved with Colonel Chechnikov and the Project Wormwood?”

The general’s face flushed with embarrassment, “How did you learn about Project Wormwood? That has nothing to do with the military intelligence, why are you asking?”

“Father, I need to know because of information I have received.”

“Well son, it is not such a secret project that you can't know. It began about eight and a half years ago. Colonel Chechnikov and your uncle Jerrod came to see me, and asked me to take part in a humanitarian project named wormwood. I don't know why it's called that. Because of my high profile position in the military, they thought I could be an effective spokesperson for the project, which was to raise the awareness throughout the world of the dangers in proliferation of nuclear weapons to other nations, world hunger, and redistribution of wealth and resources of the few wealthy nations to the third world nations. Forgiving the debt of third world nations to allow them to grow economically and most seriously, to begin a serious nuclear disarmament of missile warheads, of the United States and Russia, and also to raise the awareness of the injustice being suffered for so many years by the Palestinian peoples in the Middle East."

"I and your uncle Jerrod have been speaking at rallies and conventions all over the world for eight years. Other members of the project have been arranging peaceful demonstrations in large cities of key countries of the world. I just recently returned from America where I was invited to address the UN Security Council. Colonel Chechnikov and Jerrod are the coordinators of the project, and I am the only military official from our government that is involved. That is all there is to the project son. Now why don't you tell me what you have heard." said General Roskov.

Erik began and told his father all the information and the suspicions he had, but he did not reveal his position with the British intelligence agency. He told him about the warehouse, the overturned truck, the radioactive material, the suspicions he had about Sid's death, the missiles that struck Otto's cabin. At this point his father interrupted him with a trembling voice, "I don't know how that happened. That renegade Chechnikov almost had you killed. I have reprimanded him for that and I can assure you nothing like that will ever happen again. The information you have given me helps make my decision easy. I'm going to pull the plug and shut down the project the colonel has gotten out of control. I will call Jerrod, and tell him of my decision. I know he will remind me that he is my dear departed wife's brother, but it will not do any good. I intend to shut down the project and remove the colonel from the department of the International Space Station agency, and reassign him to a field position outside of Moscow."

Erik was so relieved to discover that his father and his Uncle Jerrod was not involved in any criminal activity, but now he had to consider how his uncle Jerrod was involved in the project. Erik left his father's office with a great deal to think about. Instead of returning to his own office, he drove to the television studio to talk to Bill. Bill had not come to the studio today, and no one at the studio had heard from him.

Chapter 38

“Good morning, and welcome to the Bill Forno show.” the announcer said. “Bill has taken a short leave of absence, due to a family emergency. For the next few weeks we will be running some of the best of Bill's morning shows, so just sit back and relax and watch some of the shows you may have missed the first time around.”

Dan had hoped they could keep their viewing audience by rebroadcasting some of Bill’s earlier shows, while he began searching for Bill, or at least hear from him.

“All passengers boarding international flight number 586 to Holland, Rome. Final destination to England, please board your plane now at gate 201B in international concourse B.” the announcer said.

“Bill, you haven't told me why you decided to take a vacation trip abroad, with absolutely no notice whatsoever?” Bill's wife said as they boarded the plane bound to England. “We had to take Jenny out of school, and she will have a lot of work to make up when we return home. You haven't even told us how long we will be gone. You just said pack enough clothes for two weeks. When we get on the plane you're going to have to give me a full explanation.”

“I will,” Bill said, “just as soon as we're on our way to England.”

The big Airbus jet began to move back from the gate, and Bill was nervously looking out the window. He turned to his wife sitting next to him and said, “Honey, I didn't want to tell you, that you and Jenny’s lives are in danger, until we were on our way to England.”

Bill then told his wife about the pictures of Jenny and her, and about the threats he had received. Bill's wife and his daughter Jenny were completely stunned by what they heard. Then Jenny began crying as she was looking at the pictures. “What are we going to do?” Bill’s wife asked, “Can't you go to the authorities and have these people arrested and put in jail?”

“No,” Bill said, “that's just it. I don't know for sure who they are, and if they are the authorities. That's why I just had to get you and Jenny out of Russia, until I can determine who these people are and under whose authority their operating. When we arrive in England we can stay at my parent's house in the country. They hardly ever use it anymore since they have gotten older, and the kids have all left. I called ahead, so the caretaker will have everything opened and ready for our arrival. After we get settled in I will call the studio, and tell Dan I'll be gone about two weeks. Then we'll have to sit down and decide what were going to do.

Chapter 39

Erik was in his office when he received a call from the police. “Erik Roskov?” the caller asked.

“Yes this is Erik Roskov, who’s speaking?”

“This is the police. You’d better come over to your father's house as soon as you can get here. Your father has been shot.”

Erik hung up the phone immediately and raced over to his father's house, which was a two-hour drive from their office. When he arrived there were three police cars and an ambulance in the drive. Erik wondered why the ambulance was still here. It had been two hours since he got the call telling him his father had been shot. Erik rushed into the house past a policeman at the front door, and was met by a Sergeant Tanner, who told him he was the person who called. They were awaiting his arrival before removing his father's body. Erik knew then, his father was dead.

"It looks like your father took his own life. He died of a single gunshot to the head. The bullet went through the temple." Sergeant Tanner explained. "Erik, was he having any personal problems that you are aware of that would cause him to take his own life?"

"No, not that I know of," Erik said, "he just returned from a trip abroad and he seemed in high spirits, when he and I were in his office a couple of days ago."

The body was lying on a gurney covered with a sheet. Erik pulled the sheet back from his father's face and just stared in disbelief. "Where was he found?" Erik asked the sergeant.

"Sitting at his desk, his neighbor heard a gunshot about noon and came over to see if everything was all right. When he rang the doorbell no one answered and he came in. The door was unlocked, and found your father slumped over his desk. When he saw what had happened, he called the police. We arrived here at about 12:45, and I called you at one o'clock."

"There was one, thing Erik." the sergeant said, "Your father scribbled something on a piece of paper he had on his desk before he died."

"What was it?" Erik said.

The sergeant called to one of his officers, “Carl bring that piece of paper that was on the general's desk.” The officer handed the piece of paper to the sergeant, who handed it to Erik. Erik looked at the paper. There was one word scribbled on it, “revelation.”

“Any idea what it means?” said the sergeant.

“No, I don't have any idea, but I want a complete and thorough investigation of the scene.”

“We will give you our complete report when we're finished.” the sergeant said.

Erik had so much to think about. He wondered if his meeting and questioning of his father about the wormwood project could have had anything to do with his father taking his life.

Erik returned to his office and called Otto to tell him the sad news. “Otto,” Erik said, “I just came from my father’s house. He has been shot. The police believe he took his own life.”

“Do you think it was self-inflicted Erik?”

“I don’t know Otto. Do you think he could have been murdered and set up to look like a suicide?”

“I don't know Erik, but I don't think your father was the kind of man to take his own life.”

“You’re right Otto.” Erik said. “Father had no reason to take his life. I am going to conduct my own investigation, and if it leads anywhere near the wormwood project and the colonel, I'm going to shut down the whole thing, and arrest all the ranking tier members, starting with the colonel."

Erik called his uncle Jerrod, and gave him the tragic news. Jerrod said he would fly to Russia at once. Erik met his uncle at the airport the following day, and on the way to Erik's apartment in the city, Erik told Jerrod about the meeting he had with his father, and asked him about the colonel and Project Wormwood. Jerrod confirmed what the general had told Erik about their involvement with the project.

While Erik and his uncle were discussing Project Wormwood, the sergeant from the investigation of his father's death called and asked Erik if he could stop in at his office sometime tomorrow. He had turned up something interesting that he would like to talk to Erik about.

Erik arrived at the police station with his uncle the following morning about 10:00. They were shown into the office of Sergeant Tanner who was on the phone. He motioned with his hand for them to be seated, when he hung up the phone. The sergeant stood up, walked around his desk and said, "Erik I'm glad you came early." He reached out his hand to Erik. "And who is this?"

"This is my uncle from England. He is my father's brother-in-law. I called him as soon as I was told about my father. He and my father were very close."

“I'm pleased meet you.” the sergeant politely said, “I had rather it been under more pleasant circumstances.”

“Erik, this is what I wanted to tell you about.” The sergeant was holding a file folder in his hand. “This is the report of what we uncovered at the scene, and at our police lab. We uncovered some interesting and troubling evidence during our investigation. We did a routine residual gunpowder test on your father's hand, to determine if your father fired a weapon, it is a test we always do when someone fires a weapon that opens an investigation. We discovered to our surprise there was no residual gunpowder. Not even in trace amounts on your fathers hand, and by that there is only one conclusion, your father did not fire the weapon he was holding in his hand.”

“Another interesting piece of evidence turned up in our investigation, when an autopsy was performed, a bullet was retrieved from your father's brain. If the weapon had been held against his head when the trigger was pulled, due to the caliber of the weapon, it would have sent the bullet completely through and into the wall. We also discovered when we ran a ballistics test on the bullet. The bullet that killed your father was not fired from the weapon he was holding. Furthermore, it had to have been fired from at least six feet away. Since the bullet that we found was the same caliber as your father's weapon, I did a little investigating and found that the type and caliber of weapon your father was holding was only issued to Soviet military officers, and were very unique. The end of the barrel was machine threaded so a silencer could be screwed onto it. Before each weapon was issued to an officer it was discharged, and the rifling marks of the bullet of each individual weapon was kept in the file of the officer to whom it was issued."

"When you came into the office I was on the phone with control files and they confirmed that a First Lieutenant Ivan Roskov was issued one of these weapons, but by crosschecking the bullet that killed your father with all other weapons issued to officers, they found that this bullet was fired from a weapon issued to a Lieutenant Ivan Chechnikov. My men went to the space station agency to arrest him, but he was not at his office. We have an all points bulletin out for him. I wanted you to know your father's death was not suicide but homicide."

"There is one thing that still troubles me." the sergeant said. "The neighbor said he only heard one shot, but your father's gun was tested and it had been fired. We are looking over the crime scene now to see if we can find the other bullet. I'll let you know if we turn up anything, and I will let you know as soon as we have Chechnikov in custody. The records show he is now a full bird colonel but we will get him.

Erik and Jerrod were still grieving over the general's death, but they were relieved to know that it was not suicide. That night Erik got a call from Sergeant Tanner. "Erik, we found the other bullet that was fired from your father's weapon. It was in the floor. Whoever shot him fired his weapon into the floor, and covered it over with a small rug. We now believe the reason the neighbor only heard one shot fired is because the gun that killed the general, was fitted with a silencer. The shot heard, was the general's gun being fired into the floor to appear as though it was the weapon that killed the general."

"Thank you Sergeant," Erik said, "and let me know as soon as you have the colonel in custody.

Erik sent intelligence agents to round up all the members of the project and bring them in for questioning. He also placed two undercover agents at the International Space Station agency, to arrest the colonel if he showed up there.

Erik learned upon questioning all the project members, which they believed they were working for a project that was sanctioned by the Russian government to peacefully bring about world peace. Since General Ivan Roskov a well respected military officer and Colonel Chechnikov, the military officer overseeing the International Space Station agency, were in the top leadership positions.

After Erik laid his dear father to rest, with a full and elaborate state funeral, Jerrod left Russia and returned home to England. Since the military agency had taken over the operations of the International Space Station agency and the colonel was in hiding, Otto and Greta believed it was safe enough for them to move out of the safe house, and moved into Otto's new cabin, which he had just finished rebuilding with the compensation that he received from the military. They had a civil wedding performed, believing Thomas was either dead, or had left Russia and gone underground.

Chapter 40

It was near the end of December, the weather in Florida at Cape Canaveral was mild. Reporters from the leading television, newspaper, and radio were there to report the first mission of the space shuttle in two years. It had been over two years since the last space shuttle had disintegrated upon reentry into the atmosphere, and all the astronauts were killed. The shuttle program was put on hold by NASA until a full investigation could determine the cause of the destruction, and a consequent redesign of the shuttle.

The International Space Station, for the past two years, had been under the control of the Russians, and inhabited by Russian cosmonauts and scientists. Completely without any oversight by the American government or NASA.

"Mission control," the flight engineer said, "all systems are a go we are ready for lift off."

"Mark ten, nine, eight, seven, six, five, four, three, two, one, we have ignition. The shuttle is on its way to the International space Station." All the reporters present, shielded their eyes from the sun as they pointed their cameras skyward, and watched the new redesigned space shuttle soar heavenward for the first time in over two years. America was back in the space-age, which it had dominated for so many years.

"Mission control this is the commander of the space shuttle." the voice said, "We have arrived at the International Space Station on schedule, and we are maneuvering into our docking position. Will advise when docking is complete." At mission control, applause broke out and there were smiles and congratulations all around.

Day five, the shuttle is scheduled to leave the space station and return to earth. "Mission control we have a problem." the voice of the commander said to the flight engineer at the controls. "Something is not working on the docking mechanism. We are unable to separate the shuttle from the dock. We have tried a number of maneuvers with no success, please advise. Standing by."

All of a sudden there was a massive hustle inside the command center. All the monitors were buzzing with information. After two full days and nights of trying to solve the problem, the flight engineer radioed to the shuttle commander. "We have instructed you to try every procedure that the computers developed and nothing has succeeded in the undocking of the shuttle from the space station. Therefore we are preparing another shuttle mission, and sending a crew of mechanics and engineers to assist you. The shuttle launch will take place in 72 hours, weather permitting. If our crew of mechanics and engineers are unable to dislodge your shuttle from the space station in 48 hours after arrival, all astronauts, engineers, and American personnel on the space shuttle are to board the second shuttle and return to earth."

The State Department and the President had been notified, and briefed of the situation. "Awaiting arrival of second shuttle the shuttle," commander said, "acknowledge your instructions."

It had been 12 hours since the second shuttle was launched, without any media present. NASA did not want the public to know the situation at the space station. Everyone in Washington was preparing for Christmas which was less than a week away. All the officials in government would be leaving Washington in a couple days and would not return until after the New Year.

Chapter 41

A clerk delivered the mail to the Secretary of State's office about 11 A.M. The aide at the reception's desk said, “All mail for Madame Secretary is to go to the Undersecretary of state's office for review, until she returns in January.”

The clerk then took the mail, and went down the hall to the Undersecretary's office. Delivering it to the aide sitting at the desk, there was a manila envelope addressed to the Secretary of State United States of America and marked personal, with bold underlined letters. Under that it was marked urgent. She immediately delivered the envelope to the Undersecretary, and returned to her desk.

The Secretary of State was arriving at the parking garage at Dulles International Airport when her cell phone rang. “Only two people on earth know this number,” she thought, “the President and the Undersecretary.”

“Hello, Mr. President and Merry Christmas to you and your family. This is not the President, Madame Secretary it’s me. I just received a message addressed to you marked urgent, so I opened it and read it, as you instructed me to do. Madam Secretary I think you need to cancel your flight and return to the capital. I believe you'll want to conference with the President.”

“If it is that urgent my Christmas plans can be changed. I will return to the Capitol at once. I should be there in about two and a half hours. Meet me in my office and have the message with you.”

The Undersecretary of State was sitting in the Secretary of State's office when she arrived from the airport. He waited until she removed her coat, hung it up, and sat down behind her desk, before he handed her the document that was sent in a manila envelope, with no return address. The postmark indicated it originated in the country of Syria.

The Secretary of State perused the document looking up at her undersecretary ever so often, and then she said, “Do we know anything about this Colonek Chechnikov?”

“I have been making inquiries since I talked to you Madame Secretary. I have learned through department channels that he is a colonel in the former Soviet Union army, and that he is presently assigned to oversee the Russian space station agency. I've also made inquiries to the CIA, but nothing has come back yet."

"Do you think it is real or some kind of terrible hoax?" the secretary said to her subordinate.

"I don't know what to think Madame Secretary. No one outside of this government, and only a few high-level Russian government officials know about the trouble at the space station with our shuttle, and our second shuttle we launched to rescue it."

"Have you contacted the president?"

"No, I want to let you make that decision."

"He has probably left the Oval Office for the holidays. I will call him at his ranch tonight." the Secretary said. "I want you to find out everything you can, and I will contact the Russian President, and see what he knows. You get over to the CIA's office and instruct them to inquire through all of their back channels, to all of their field operators and see how much, if anything we can learn, before I talk to the President tonight."

"Don't let anyone over there hinder you from collecting data. Let them know this is a national emergency."

The response by the director of the CIA was quick and thorough. All foreign agencies were contacted through back channel resources. All CIA foreign operations were contacted, and instructed to inquire of all their field agents to find out anything they could or anything they had heard about Colonel Chechnikov, or Project Wormwood.

The information started coming in about 1:00 P.M. that afternoon. “There had been an interest in Colonel Chechnikov for about eight and a half years. The chatter on the internet was, that he was leading a group of environmental protesters, to demonstrate against a whole array of environmental issues, throughout the world. No one has been able to trace his source of income, and he has been keeping close company with a general in the Russian military. As well as a wide range of eco-scientists worldwide. In the late afternoon more information started coming in from many sources. We have learned that his father was not a Russian at all but rather he was a German. It seems that his father lived in the city of the Roel in Palestine around 1948. He had a very successful tailoring and textile business. Prior to 1948 his father and mother lived in Germany and his father ran a large successful tailoring business. One of his largest customers was the German military during the years of the Nazi rule under the dictatorship of Adolph Hitler. His father’s company had the contract to tailor all the German army’s officer's uniforms. When the war was over and the armies of Hitler were defeated, the allied forces poured into Berlin. His Father was fearful that he would be arrested by the Russian armed forces and charged as a collaborator to the enemy. He left his tailoring business and fled as many other German businessmen, to the Middle East and settled in Palestine. There he changed his name from Chechnikoff a German name, to Chechnikov a Russian name."

"His father then built a successful tailoring and textile business in Palestine. Only to be driven out in 1948 as a non-documented foreigner, when the land of Palestine was divided and given by a decree of the United Nations and world governments to the Jewish race as a homeland. He took his wife and his infant son Ivan and fled to the former Soviet Union. He was never again able to build a successful business to provide for his family. For that he had a deep hatred for the Jews."

"When Ivan Chechnikov was eight years old, his father placed him in a state run military school in the Soviet Union. It was there that he trained to become a soldier. Ivan left the military school at the age of 18, and both his father and mother died before he was 20 years old. When he was 21 years old attending a Soviet University, he became very interested and involved in the eco-sciences. So much so that he left the university and joined an ecology group called Green Planet."

We know that the Green Glanet ecology group is a radical environmental movement with an agenda to return the western nations from large industrial environmental pollution producing nations, back into nations of agriculture as they were a hundred years ago. They staged violent demonstrations all over the world and have in recent years linked with other environmental groups to form a formidable movement."

"Ivan Chechnikov was introduced a few years ago to a professor Jerrod Stevens, from England, who is an outspoken professor on the ecology of the planet and its eco-systems. After thier introduction Ivan became the radical spokesperson for Professor Jerrod's radical agenda."

"It was a few years prior to the Kyoto conference on world ecology that Professor Jerrod and Ivan Chechnikov began recruiting from around the world prominent eco-scientists who were of the same ilk that they were."

"Ivan has been traveling throughout the world to promote these radical agendas. He and Professor Jerrod recruited a three star general from the Soviet military to be a spokesman for the movement. This general is the brother-in-law of Professor Jerrod."

"The CIA has been monitoring their movements for about eight years. Chechnikov returned to the Soviet military a few years ago, and has since rose in rank to a full colonel. He seems to have drifted away from the forefront of the movement when he was appointed by the Soviet military government to oversee the International Space Station agency in Moscow. He has recently been seen at a few of the high profile ecology conferences, and he also attended the Kyoto conference."

"That's all the information that we have on Ivan Chechnikov, but presently his primary position inside Russia has been the military overseer of the Russian space station, that has become the International Space Station, being funded by the United States. Jointly manned by United States astronauts and Russian cosmonauts, until 2 1/2 years ago when NASA put the shuttle program on hold after the disaster."

"Mr. President," the Secretary of State said, "I hesitate to bring you this devastating news, and especially to bring it to you on your holiday with your family, but something that will require your urgent attention has come up. I believe that we need you back in Washington now."

"Can we discuss it on the phone or through coded channels?"

"No Mr. President, it has to be in person. You will want some of your cabinet members and especially the Joint Chiefs of Staff back in Washington as well."

"I will be in the office at 8:00 A.M. Contact the members of my cabinet that you believe are appropriate and I will contact the Joint Chiefs of Staff. Have everyone in my office, in Washington, at 8:00 A.M."

"Consider it done Mr. President, and again I am so sorry."

When the president arrived at 7:30 A.M. the Secretary of State, Undersecretary, Director of CIA and several members of the White House security staff were already there waiting. The members of the Joint Chiefs of Staff arrived at about 8:00 A.M.

There were copies of the documents received the previous day on the table before each person present. Realizing that the President had not yet seen the document the Secretary of State said, "Sir would you like me to begin the briefing?"

"Go ahead, I'm listening."

"Gentlemen," the Secretary of State said, "you have been called back to Washington because of the documents in the folders in front of each of you. First let me say I and the President are extremely sorry to have had to interrupt your holidays with your families."

"There are a few things you need to know before you read the document. First we do not know who sent it, and second we have not yet been able to determine if it is a hoax. Third when you read it be aware it is highly classified, and that is the reason you see no aides or stenographer's in this meeting. All the briefing is being video taped, and is classified as top-secret."

“Now each of you may read the document.” A short pause happen in the room then the Secretary of State said, “This document was delivered by first-class mail to my office just before noon yesterday. It was in a plain manila envelope with no return address.”

“The postal markings on the envelope seemed to indicate that it was sent from someone in Syria. Since receiving it, we have learned very little about the author. As you can see we have only 48 hours to carry out the instructions it contains. Before I read the document aloud, let me remind you that not more than six of us in this room had previous knowledge of the rescue shuttle that was sent to the International Space Station.”

“Therefore, most of you are learning about it from this document. Each of you will remain in the loop to receive all intelligence information we receive until this is resolved. No members of Congress have yet been notified. The President and I will do that at the appropriate time.”

“Now if I can have your undivided attention, I will read the document aloud, and then I will ask for any comments you may have, beginning with you Mr. President.”

“To the honorable Madame Secretary of State, of the United States of America, greetings from an avid admirer, Colonel Ivan Chechnikov, officer of the Soviet people, I will keep this message to your Government brief, but you must understand it is no less urgent and sincere. I am certain by the time you receive this message you will know that both of your space shuttles are being held hostage at our space station. Along with all American crew members. To learn why and what it will cost to release them, you must assemble all the top leaders of every nation, represented on the UN Security Council. They must be assembled within the next 48 hours in the chambers of the UN Security Council."

"In exactly 60 hours from the time you receive this message, I will speak to all of you on a closed satellite link. At that time I will reveal to you our concerns, and also our demands. I am assuming you are meeting at the White House today, Saturday morning, if you are you have only 48 hours to contact and assemble all the world leaders that we spoke of."

"To give them an incentive to participate, you can tell them that we have nuclear weapons, and they have been strategically placed and aimed at many of their nations. I will meet with you at the UN Security Council chambers in exactly 48 hours, Signed Colonel Ivan Chechnikov, The People's Supreme Commander of a peaceful world."

No one spoke. There was complete silence in the room. Then the president said, "Gentlemen we are considering this as gravely serious. There are to be no turf wars on gathering information. You all must use every piece of intelligence and every piece of intelligence gathering machinery and technology that you have available. All intelligence gathered will flow into the Secretary of State's office. That office will become our war room. We only have 48 hours to find out everything we can and to assemble all the world leaders. Thank you."

One of the Joint Chiefs of Staff said, "Do we have another shuttle that we can get ready for launch and send a contingent of armed military to the station, and forcibly take possession of the International Space Station, and bring our people and our two shuttles' home?"

"No, we do not." the Secretary of State said. "If we did we would never be allowed to dock at the space station.

One of the cabinet members said, "When will the congressional leaders be notified and how long can this be kept from the public?"

The President stood at the end of the conference table and said, "The members of Congress or the news media will not have any knowledge of this situation until after the meeting with the UN members of the Security Council, and world leaders. Any leaks that come out of this room, will be considered a treasonable offense, and the person or persons that leak any information that they have learned in this meeting, or that they learned through intelligence gathering will be considered a traitor to the United States government and will be prosecuted to the full extent of the law."

"If you need to use wiretaps, to gather intelligence within the next 48 hours, the Attorney General will authorize them. Whatever resources you need will be made available to you with no red tape. I will sign an executive order, to protect you, and to prevent any of you or your contacts from ever being prosecuted for illegal activities concerning this intelligence gathering mission. And you will all be protected under the homeland security act, as a national security operation. Now this meeting is adjourned, we have only 48 hours."

The President sat down in the Oval Office, and picked up the red phone on his desk. He had never used it before, nor had he any reason to since the cold war between the United States and Russia had long been over. The phone rang once, and the Russian President said, "What is the urgency Mr. President?" After the President briefed the Russian President he requested that he send his department head of military intelligence to Washington immediately. He agreed.

Chapter 42

Erik was enjoying the Christmas season at the new cabin Otto had built, with Otto and Greta when his cell phone rang. “Erik,” the caller said, “this is the President. I need to know where you are at this moment, so I can send a military helicopter to pick you up and take you to a special plane that is waiting to fly you to Washington D.C. I will brief you of your mission when you are in flight to United States.”

Erik said, “Yes of course Mr. President. I will be at a clearing, at the following coordinates.” Then Erik gave the President the coordinates where he could be picked up by the helicopter.

“They will be there in 30 minutes. I will talk to you when you're in flight to the United States, until then goodbye.”

“What is it?” Otto said.

“I don't know, but it sounds mysterious and urgent. I won't have time to return to my office, or my apartment. I am being sent to Washington in the United States on a mission for the President. Otto I may ask you to send me some personal things from my apartment when I get to Washington. Here is the key, and also my office key is on there as well. In case I need any of my files to be sent to me in Washington.”

Erik left Otto and Greta and met the helicopter at the rendezvous, and was flown to the awaiting plane. Then he was on his way to Washington in less than an hour. It was a long flight for Erik, and the first time he had ever been to the United States. The Russian President briefed him of his mission in flight as he said he would. Erik told the President that he had arranged with Otto to send him all his files he would need in Washington. He would call Otto in flight and tell him what files he would need from his office, and Otto could send them to him in Washington.

The Russian military jet was cleared for landing at Dulles International Airport. Upon landing Erik boarded an awaiting Presidential helicopter, which shuttled him to the White House. When the helicopter touched down at the White House, a man wearing a pair of khaki pants, dressed very casually, met Erik with his hand outstretched. Erik assumed he was one of the American Presidents aides welcoming him to Washington. “Mr. Roskov I am the President of the United

States. Your President has briefed me on your arrival. Follow me and we will get right to work."

The President and Erik walked into the Oval Office, and were greeted by two members of the Joint Chiefs of Staff and the Secretary of State. "Thank you for coming on such short notice." the Secretary of State said as she handed Erik a file folder marked classified and top secret. "We understand that you probably know more about the person who sent this message than anyone else."

Erik opened the folder and briefly perused the file. "Yes I probably do," said Erik, "and he is a very dangerous man. He is capable of carrying out any threat he makes. Where would you like me to start? I can't give you specific dates until my files arrive, but I can give you some important details about this man."

"We want to know everything you know Erik," the President said, "but we want that briefing done over at the State Department in our war room." The whole entourage then moved from the Oval Office in the White House, over to the State Department to the war room. All the rest of the members that had attended the meeting were there awaiting Erik's arrival. The President said, "Erik I want you to tell us everything that you know about Colonel Chechnikov, and his role in the International Space Station. Don't leave out the smallest detail. Because it may be important to learn what this is all about."

"I will give you as much information as I can remember, or that I know." Erik said. As he sat down at the end of a large conference table in the war room at the State Department all eyes were fixed upon this curly red haired Russian. They gave him their undivided attention.

After two hours of revealing everything he knew about the colonel and Project Wormwood, beginning with Greta and then with Otto, and all they had found out. Including the warehouse in the mountains, the radioactive material being sent by the truck, all the additional food and water supplies being loaded in the cargo hold to be sent to the Russian space station, and all the details that he could remember, including the death of his good friend Sid, and the details they uncovered about his father's death, and the word "revelation" that he scribbled on the pad before his death. Then Erik looked at the President, "Mr. President, will I be given clearance to attend the meeting at the UN?"

"You not only will have clearance Erik, but we are counting on your briefing to assist us in assembling all the world leaders to that meeting." Then the President stood at the head of the table, "What was that word again Erik that your father scribbled on the pad, before he died?"

“It was just one word, revelation. I have no idea what it meant or what he was trying to say.”

The President then thought for a moment, “The only thing that comes to my mind is a book in our Christian Bibles New Testament. It's called a book of Revelation. Now maybe there is something in that book that is relative to what we are experiencing now. We'll look at it more thoroughly later.”

Chapter 43

The 48 hour deadline was just minutes away, all the Security Council members were present and most of the world leaders that were contacted were present in the UN council chambers when the president and the Secretary of State and all their entourage entered the chamber. Everyone was buzzing, all the world leaders that had been drawn from their holidays with their families, and had come from all over the world to this special meeting because of its urgency, and the threat of a nuclear attack upon their nations.

All eyes were fixed upon three giant screens, waiting for them to come to life. It had not been easy to convince some of the world leaders that this was not just an American problem. When the nuclear equation entered the discussion, along with Erik's briefing, they recognized it as a world problem. The clock ticked off the minutes ten, nine, eight, seven, six, five, four, three, two, one, and suddenly the giant screens lit up and came to life. Colonel Chetchnikov stood at the dais with a large world map in the background. Several other men were seated just outside of the camera's range.

"Gentlemen I am glad you could all come to this most important meeting. Let me introduce myself and one of my colleagues that will be addressing you today. I am Colonel Chechnikov, officer of the Soviet Union, and people's supreme commander of a peaceful world." Then one of the men sitting in the shadows stood up and came forward to the dais. "This is my dear friend and faithful colleague Professor Jerrod, from England." Erik could hardly believe his eyes, this was his Uncle Jerrod. Whom he had trusted and loved but Erik said nothing.

"What is going to be revealed here today gentlemen," the Colonel continued, "is what my colleagues and I refer to, as Project Wormwood. We chose that name because of its similarity to the Christian Bible account in the book of Revelation, which is recorded in the eighth, chapter of the book. We have been developing this plan to secure a peaceful co-existence with all nations of the world. It has taken over ten years to develop this plan. Now we finally have everything in place that we need to fulfill our plan, which we refer to as Project Wormwood."

"I will, for now, yield the floor to my dear friend and colleague. Who will outline in detail the plan that will ultimately bring peace to the whole world."

Professor Jerrod stepped up to the dais as the Colonel took a seat behind him. The tall well dressed man gazed into the camera and gave a formal and friendly greeting. Then with a laser pointer in his hand he began to reveal the details of Project Wormwood. The delegates and world leaders from nearly every nation sat quietly and attentive, they knew what they were about to hear, why they had been intimidated to attend this gathering.

Professor Jerrod began to speak in a low monotone voice as he pointed his laser pointer toward maps, which an aide turned at his command. "My colleagues and I have been extremely concerned over the past ten years at what we have seen in every nation on this planet. We have seen heavily armed mobs in many nations, sanctioned by their governments, killing and raping their fellow citizens, while looting and burning their homes, only because they were of different ethnic heritage. More genocide has been sanctioned by governments, in the last 20 years, than all the atrocities that were performed by the Nazis, in World War II."

"Also, we have witnessed industrial holocaust carried out by a handful of western and European nations, which is bringing rapid destruction to our planet. These few nations are raping and destroying the entire eco-system of this planet. It began with the deletion of the ozone layer, which is the only protection this planet and its life forces have against the deadly ultra-violet rays, emanating from our sun. The destruction of the ozone layer allows the ultraviolet rays from the sun to penetrate our earth and destroy its natural habitat. This pollution and destruction of our planet's life giving eco-system, by a few nations, at the expense of the remaining two thirds of the population of our planet, has brought about catastrophic conditions through out the world. We have seen global warming in the last 20 years, which we tried to address at the Kyoto conference with little success, which has caused ice burgs to break off in the Antarctica, as large as the state of Maryland of the United States. The pollution that these nations are pumping into the atmosphere has caused climate changes in every region of the world. The acid rain which is produced by these industrialized giants has destroyed millions of acres of forestry all over the planet. It has destroyed what was fertile agricultural land and turned it into desert. Whole countries have lost their agricultural livelihood, because their crops will no longer grow due to radical climate changes brought about by global warming. This wanton destruction of our planet's eco-system has escalated the past 10 years to a degree that we can no longer tolerate. It is for this reason that a large body of eco-scientists from all over the world has decided that the only way this destruction can be stopped, is through the threat of nuclear destruction. All nations of this planet will ultimately be affected. We decided that we can no longer stand idly by while a handful of economically wealthy nations exploit 85 to 90 percent of this world's natural resources. To force feed their economies at the expense of two thirds of the population of our planet, made up of all the third world nations, whose people are starving and killing each other nemeses. In the worst cases of genocide this world has ever known. Not only do these few wealthy nations control and exploit the largest share of the earth's natural resources, such as the oil, gas, timber, minerals, and even the larger share of the food sources of this planet."

"Because these few nations control over 90% of the agricultural land on this planet, they are able to use food as an intimidating weapon against the struggling poor nations. Their populations who are either starving or near starvation. While these few nations economies are running at high speed and their populations are becoming fatter and richer, two thirds of the population of the earth is falling farther and farther behind economically. Their children are dying of starvation by the millions daily. Wars, diseases, and poverty are killing millions everyday. Therefore it is time for the inequities of this earth's populations to end."

“We have not only seen all of this, and just wrung our hands in despair, but we have developed a broad world plan to change the course of the history of mankind. To change the course of mankind on this planet, will require ultra radical changes.”

“The following solutions have been thought out very carefully by all the eco-scientists that are participating in Project Wormwood. These are the requirements that will change the world. Number one, every nation must be disarmed of nuclear weapons, and the development and research of chemical and biological weapons of mass destruction must be terminated. Also every nation must dismantle all their armed forces, and recall all military machinery and personnel back to their country of origin, including all sea going vessels. All chemical, biological, and nuclear weapons must then be destroyed, never to be used again on any nation or any peoples. Also, every nation will collect and destroy all personal, private, and government controlled weapons of any kind. Number two, all outstanding debts owed to World Bank's and developed nations in the world by third world countries will be forgiven. These third world countries may begin to see their economies move forward and their people prosper. Also a redistribution of all the earth's land and resources will be mandated and equally divided among earth's populations. Number three, the borders surrounding every nation will cease to exist, allowing every citizen of the earth to live and work and recreate any place on this planet where he or she chooses. Number four, because of the illegal recognition by the world leaders of all the peoples that call themselves Jews, which took place in 1948, and perpetrated an injustice upon the Palestinian people."

"They were robbed of their homeland, and driven into the desert and wilderness areas of their region. To give these few recognized peoples a homeland in Palestine, there will be a special allotment granted to the Palestinian people. All documented Israelites will be removed from the land of Palestine, and dispersed throughout the world, allowing the Palestinian people once and for all to occupy all of their rightful land of Palestine. Number five, there will be an equal distribution of food sources and livestock throughout the world. Number six, due to the unjust inequities that have been perpetrated on the rest of the known world by the United States for over two hundred years, two thirds of the population of the United States will be exported to African nations and third world countries, leaving all their possessions and wealth behind. The reason for this severe measure being taken is because the United States, with its unparalleled and wealthy economy, is due in part we believe to the slave trade of the past centuries. We believe this economy was built on the backs of African slaves. Therefore all living Africans should be allowed to share in this wealth."

"Thank you gentlemen for listening, and again let me say how very sorry we all are that we have to take these radical measures to save this planet for all future generations. Now I will return the floor to Colonel Chechnikov who will explain to you how these changes will be implemented, and also the consequences of Project Wormwood on the nations of the world if they are not."

"Thank you, Professor Jerrod." the Colonel said as he approached the dais. "We will pause in our presentation for 30 minutes. We will resume our presentation in exactly 30 minutes, so do not be late, there is much more information to come." The giant screens went dark in the conference room.

At first there was a deafening silence in the room, and then it seemed that all the world leaders began talking at once. They were unaware that each of them was speaking in their native tongue, and none of the others could understand what they were saying.

Then one of the leaders stood and said, as he motioned with his hands to put on the headphones that were provided at each station, that each person that wanted to speak to the rest of the body should do so from their microphones. The electronic equipment would automatically translate all speech into each ones own language.

They all agreed, and put on the head phones. Each one spoke in turn in an orderly fashion.

First the Russian President spoke. It was a very moving speech lasting for 5 minutes. He humbly apologized for the lack of security over the nuclear arsenals in the old Soviet Union when the States were dismantled, under his predecessor. He also was sorry for not paying more attention to the oversight of the space station, which had he done, this may never have occurred.

Then the President of the United States spoke for 15 minutes. After that, as many leaders that had time before the 30 minutes was up, asked many pointed questions. They all expressed their sorrow for the American personnel that were being held hostage at the space station.

After 30 minutes the satellite feed was resumed and the screens came to life. The Colonel was at the dais beginning to speak.

"Many of you are probably thinking, after hearing Professor Jerrod outline the changes that you all must make, there is no possible way for these changes to be implemented in your respective sovereign nations. Let me assure you, there is a way, and I'm going to tell you how."

"To help in the implementation of our plan, we have solicited the assistance of one nation on earth, that nation is the Republic of China. Their government has agreed to put in place one billion armed military soldiers and to place them under our command. We have already begun to draw up plans setting forth orders for that nation and their one billion armed forces. They are ready to be deployed and assemble throughout the earth, in every nation at our command. They will be armed with all the strategic weapons, including nuclear, biological, and chemical laden warheads that are needed for this task."

"We have also appointed a military statesman, from a Middle Eastern country, to build and establish a world headquarters in the city of Jerusalem in Palestine. We believe since that city, more than any other city in the world, has been the flashpoint for more hostility in the whole world, than any other place, it is appropriate for that city to house the world headquarters for peace. Shortly the construction of the world headquarters will begin construction. It will be built on the site of the Jews sacred Temple Mount, where there stands now the Islamic Holy Temple, and several other buildings. This temple and these other structures will be dismantled and moved to a new location. There will be nothing occupying that site with the exception of the world headquarters. This world headquarters will be the place in which the Imperial Commander of earth's people will command and control all the populations of earth."

“Since the people in all lands are either superstitious or religious we feel it is necessary to establish a new world religion. A new temple will be erected on the Holy Temple Mount in Jerusalem, and in that temple will be placed designated priests and high priests out of every religious order with the exception of Christianity. Christianity in will be abolished forever from the face of this planet, because it is through Christianity that more bloodshed and more hostility and more destruction of our planet and its peoples have occurred in the last two millenniums. Anyone practicing or condoning Christianity will be annihilated without trial including men women and children. All of their possessions will be confiscated by the religious leaders of the new world religion and distributed to the poor throughout the earth.”

“By this time you are probably thinking, how this madman thinks he is going to deploy an army onto our sovereign shores and across our borders. To occupy our nations and have every nation lay down their arms abdicating our authority to him. Well, I'm going to let a colleague of mine, on the International Space Station, tell you exactly how we're going to accomplish it, without firing one shot.”

Screeeeeech, the satellite feed was disrupted for a moment and then a new face appeared on the screens.

“Gentlemen, let me introduce myself to you at this time. My name is Dr. Haunce Weber. I am well-known as a nuclear physicist, a doctor of science technology, and an expert on earth's eco-systems. Many of you in this room probably will recognize me from when I spoke and warned the nations of the world at the Kyoto conference a few years ago. At that conference we were unable to convince the large industrialized nations, such as the United States and England, to agree to cut the pollution from their factories, which was causing world wide temperature changes. They, along with some other nations, did not believe in the global warming scenario we presented. It was after that conference, and the blatant disregard for the earth's eco-systems, that my colleagues and I decided we must do something to save the planet, and all life forces."

"For 25 years of my life I have studied the eco-systems of the world, and their interaction with earth's natural forces and all forms of life forces including humanity. These forces have co-existed and worked together harmoniously for over 6 million years, that is until the last 100 years. In the last 100 years the balance of nature has been disrupted in a most incomprehensible way by humanity."

"It is for this reason that I have quietly recruited many of the most noted eco-scientists of the world, from every nation, to join with me to develop this plan. We call Project Wormwood, and it must be implemented now, before it's too late to save this earth."

"Our project members, in the past five years, have covertly located a large number of nuclear warhead missiles in many strategic locations on this planet. Thanks in part to the lack of security of the nuclear arsenals of the Soviet Union, when that great body of states was dismantled. Every intercontinental ballistic missile we have under our control is armed with multiple warheads, which are set to target many of the most populated and industrialized cities on this planet."

"If the requirements that we have outlined before you today, for changing this planet and its populations, are rejected by any nation, we will not hesitate to deploy one or more of these nuclear missiles on to these nations. Totally annihilate them from our planet. It would be with heavy hearts that we would take this necessary action, but we understand it is the only way. To sacrifice the few for the many, we can save this planet."

"We have here on the International Space Station, where I am broadcasting from, two American space shuttles. Which when redeployed to the earth, are capable of entering the atmosphere at any predetermined location. These shuttles are being loaded with deadly nerve gas, biological and nuclear warheads, and other nuclear devices which will be preset to detonate at a given altitude and or at a preset atmospheric pressure. They cannot be destroyed without destroying the earth."

"If the requirements of our project are rejected by any Pacific Rim nation, the United States or the European Union nations, we will deploy these deadly chemical, biological and nuclear loaded shuttles, to target the Pacific Rim and the United States. Upon entering the earth's atmosphere these shuttles will target the largest industrialized nations. They will release deadly chemicals and biological warheads in strategic places on the earth, and poison much of the earth's fresh water supply. Then they will enter the Pacific and Atlantic Oceans at a point chosen by us, and the nuclear devices within them are designed to detonate in the water, at a depth which will produce deadly earthquakes. We calculate will be in the range of a nine or ten on the Richter scale. Also it will cause tsunamis of 100 feet high, traveling at a speed across the ocean at 400 kilometers an hour. They will reach temperatures in excess of 600 degrees Fahrenheit. They will be traveling toward the Pacific and Atlantic coasts. When they reach the shores of these Pacific Rim nations and the Atlantic coasts, millions of people will be killed and thousands of cities will be destroyed."

"My colleagues and I are very saddened that we have to take these extreme measures to save this planet. Thank you for your attention and you're ultimate cooperation, and now I will sign off."

Screeeeeech! The satellite feed was lost again momentarily then the Colonel reappeared on the screens.

"Gentlemen, as you've just heard we are deadly serious about implementing Project Wormwood. Now that you have learned it is not an option or choice to participate in our plan, but rather it is mandatory for all nations. Let me give you the blue print of the plan, and exactly what will be required to ensure world peace."

"Once our world government is set in place with its headquarters in Jerusalem, our project teams will be sent to every major city of the world. With the Chinese forces which will be spread throughout the world, and the restructured United Nations, we will begin to register every citizen on the earth. This will require every citizen to be brought to a registration office in the country in which they are abiding, and be implanted with an electronic coded number. This barcode number will be placed by an electronic devise, and it can neither be altered nor removed. If it is altered or anyone tries to remove it from their body it will self destruct and kill the person in which it is implanted instantly. It will be implanted in his or her hand or in their forehead. It can be scanned each time they need to renew their supplies or they need to conduct any business, including buying or selling food. This electronic code will be entered into an international database, and when every citizen of the earth is registered, which we believe can be done in less than one year, the World Government will then take control of all the worlds industry of all commerce of all communication, energy and food supplies."

"Every citizen of the earth will then be measured just enough of all the world's resources, including food, shelter, and energy to live a comfortable life anywhere they choose, as long as it is approved by our committee on human affairs. On a predetermined basis each individual or family will be allotted just what they have need of month by month. All of these resources can only be accessed by their registration code."

"My colleagues and I know that there will be pockets of resistance to the registration code, and some citizens of earth will refuse to have the electronic chip implanted. These renegades of resistance will be dealt with in a harsh manner. We know that they will have stockpiles of needed resources in many places, but they will be limited."

"Those citizens who resist registering with the world headquarters will only be left with the alternative to flee into the mountains and wilderness areas of the world. And these pockets of resistance will be hunted down and destroyed by the armed forces that are deployed by the United Nations. Not only will the men, but also the women and children be killed without any trial."

"There may indeed be some which will elude our armed forces for some time. However, they will be unable to purchase any goods or services anywhere on earth through the World Government, because they will not have been registered in our database."

"Gentlemen, I know the ten hours you have been here and listening to what changes must be implemented has been very tiring. I only have one more part of our plan to share with you, please be patient."

"The financial costs to implement these changes will be enormous. It will require in the first 12 months of operation to receive taxation from every nation. It will begin with the United States. The United States will be required to contribute to the World Government 100 billion dollars in the first 12 months. The European Union states and countries will be required to contribute equal amounts, and the amounts for the rest of the nations will be revealed to them in the first 12 months."

"These contributions will be needed to finance the implementation of our plan. It will be implemented through the assistance of the United Nations and the Chinese Army. After the first 12 months all the assets of every nation on earth will be placed under the control of our one World Government."

"You all have set before you enormous tasks to prepare your people in your individual countries for these changes. However you do so, we would suggest that you do it without creating a worldwide panic."

"My colleagues and I have set a timetable of 24 months of preparation, to give every nation time to prepare their people for these changes before we implement our plan. During the first 12 months you will be begin total disarmament, and you will also be required to withdraw all military personnel from all foreign countries and completely dismantle your military machinery. You will also be required to deemphasize and destabilize your central governmental bodies and prepare your people for the shifting of your governments to one World Government."

"We are confident that all these changes can be implemented in no less than 24 months. If these changes are implemented in every nation according to our instructions and requirements we will never have to execute Project Wormwood. The world will, for the first time in over 2000, years be at peace. And although the peace throughout the world will be tenuous at first, under the leadership and the military force of the World Government and the assistance of the Chinese armed forces and the United Nations. Together we believe that we can bring a lasting peace to this planet. Thank you gentlemen for attending this conference, and for your future cooperation, you can bring lasting peace to this planet. It is in your hands. Good day and thank you for listening."

Not a word was spoken as the giant screens went black. All the delegates at the conference center filed out of the security chambers in an orderly fashion and drove off in their waiting vehicles.

Chapter 44

That meeting took place less than six months ago. I do not know what each of these government leaders are doing to prepare their people for the inevitable changes, but I have at great risk to myself have written this book to challenge all of you to submit to these enormous demands and the changes they require. For we have no alternative and it will all to lead to peace on this earth without the implementation of Project Wormwood.

As Erik and I were in his office in Moscow conducting our last interview for this book, he noticed the icon on his computer flashing indicating that he had an e-mail message. He clicked on the icon and saw this message. "Erik, I have very little time. I am sending this message at the risk of being discovered. I am alive and well and I am hiding on the

International Space Station. I have overheard the plans that have been laid out by these mad scientist's and I am going to try with every means that I have to stop the implementation of Project Wormwood." Signed Thomas Burkov, "Please inform O'Donnel."

The end.

About The Author

Lynn D. Nelson uses a mixture of the literary style of many of the great classical authors including Edger Allen Poe and John Grissom, as well as many other.

Very early after leaving high school, Lynn was called by God into the ministry. He served for more then 40 years as a pastor, evangelist, and teacher. He raised his family in the Midwest. When his children were all gone from the home, he and his beloved wife Cathy began traveling around the country ministering. Usually to smaller out of the way church, to congregations of 300 or less. Although he continued working in the secular field, he always remained faithful to his call to the ministry.

He began writing in his latter years, although his love for writing and reading mystery novels has been his passion all his life. His current residence is still in the Midwest, where he enjoys his writing, which occupies him after the passing of his beloved wife of 49 years in 2005.